JUDI CURTIN grew up in Cork and now lives in Limerick where she is married with three children. Judi is the best-selling author of the 'Alice & Megan' series and the 'Eva' series; with Roisin Meaney, she is also the author of *See If I Care*, and she has written three novels, *Sorry, Walter*, *From Claire to Here* and *Almost Perfect*. Her books have sold into Serbian, Portuguese, German, Russian and Lithuanian, and into Australia and New Zealand.

The 'Alice & Megan' series

Alice Next Door

Alice Again

Don't Ask Alice

Alice in the Middle

Bonjour Alice

Alice & Megan Forever

Alice to the Rescue

Viva Alice!

Alice & Megan's Cookbook

Other books

Eva's Journey

Eva's Holiday

Leave it to Eva

Eva and the Hidden Diary

See If I Care (with Roisin Meaney)

Alice in the Middle

Judi Curtin

Illustrations: Woody Fox

THE O'BRIEN PRESS
DUBLIN

First published 2007 by The O'Brien Press Ltd,
12 Terenure Road East, Rathgar, Dublin 6, Ireland.
Tel: +353 1 4923333; Fax: +353 1 4922777
E-mail: books@obrien.ie
Website: www.obrien.ie
Reprinted 2008, 2009, 2011, 2012.
This edition first published 2014 by The O'Brien Press Ltd.

ISBN: 978-1-84717-673-8

1 3 5 7 8 6 4 2

14 16 18 19 17 15

Cover by Nicola Colton
Internal illustrations: Woody Fox
Layout and design: The O'Brien Press Ltd.
Printed and bound by CPI Group (UK) Ltd, Croydon, CR0 4YY
The paper used in this book is produced using pulp from managed forests.

The O'Brien Press receives financial assistance from

For Mary, Declan, Caroline and Kieran.

Thanks to all my family and friends for their ongoing support and encouragement.

Thanks also to everyone at The O'Brien Press, especially my editor, Helen.

Thanks to all the great bookshops and libraries who organised readings and signings, and to all the readers who have written me such wonderful letters about Alice and Megan.

Chapter one

I woke up and noticed that I was smiling, the way you do when you've been having a really fantastic dream. Then I realised that I hadn't been dreaming, and I smiled even more. I stretched my arms over my head, banging my knuckles hard on the wall behind my bed. That should have hurt, but I didn't feel any pain. I jumped out of bed, pulled back my curtains and looked outside. The sky was a dull grey, like the colour of Mum's favourite porridge pot. Rain was beating hard against my bedroom window, but it didn't matter. Nothing mattered today, I thought. This was going to be the most wonderful day of my whole life.

I went in to the kitchen, where Mum was stirring a pot of porridge.

'Excited?' she said.

I nodded, almost afraid to speak. Then I sat down at the table, in my usual place.

'We're going to miss you,' she said.

Suddenly the excitement got too much for me. I jumped up, raced over to Mum and hugged her hard. Then all the words I'd been afraid to say tumbled out of my mouth.

'Mum, I'm so, so, *so* excited. I'm going to summer camp and Alice is coming too and it's going to be so, so, so, *so* great and we're going to do fun stuff every day and, and, and–'

'–and you're going to miss us too?' asked Mum, wriggling free of my hug.

I shook my head, and then noticed how sad Mum looked.

'Well,' I said quickly, 'I suppose I will miss you a bit at first.'

Mum smiled.

'But not so much that you'll be phoning for Dad and me to come and take you home?'

I shook my head again.

'No way.'

Mum smiled again, but somehow managed to look sad while she was smiling.

'My little girl,' she said. 'All grown up and off to summer camp. Now sit down and eat your porridge, or you're not going anywhere.'

I was too happy to argue with her. I sat down again, and Mum put a huge bowl of porridge in front of me. I ate quickly, trying not to grin as I thought of the twenty-one wonderful porridge-free days that stretched ahead of me.

As soon as breakfast was over, I went back into my bedroom and finished off my packing. By eleven o'clock I was all ready to go. I zipped up my rucksack and carried it into the hall where

Mum was waiting for me wearing the same smiling-but-sad face.

'I'm ready,' I said. (Just in case she hadn't noticed.)

Mum took a deep breath and started on her list.

'Have you packed your toothbrush and toothpaste?'

I nodded.

'Have you got enough clean underwear?'

I nodded again. Was this conversation really necessary?

'And the new top Auntie Mona sent you?'

I nodded again, though this was a lying nod. The top Auntie Mona had sent me was totally hideous – orange and pink with big scratchy frills. It looked like a cheerleader's pom-pom gone wrong. When Mum wasn't looking I'd hidden it under my mattress.

'And plenty of warm jumpers?'

'And a good book?'

'And sunscreen?'

And a big sack of sweets and chocolate?

Mum didn't say the last one of course. Only my dream-Mum, the normal one, would ever say something like that.

And on and on she went.

'A sun hat?'

'A raincoat?'

I looked at my watch impatiently. If Mum didn't hurry up, I'd miss the bus, and then it wouldn't matter whether the five thousand things she'd mentioned were in my bag or not.

Just then the doorbell rang. Through the glass door, I could see the outline of a figure. I breathed a big sigh of relief when I realised that it was an Alice-shaped outline. Was I ever glad to see her!

I opened the door and my best friend stepped into the hallway.

'All set?' she asked. 'Have you everything packed?'

'Shhh,' I whispered, 'or you'll start Mum off again.'

Then in a louder voice I said, 'Can we go now?'

Mum nodded, with a worried look on her face. 'I suppose so. If you're sure you have everything?'

I pulled her by the arm.

'I have, I promise. Now let's go before we miss the bus.'

Dad and my little sister Rosie came downstairs, and we all climbed into our battered old car. Alice's dad stood on their front doorstep and waved goodbye.

Why couldn't I get a sensible send-off like that?

Why did my whole family have to come to see me off?

Why did I always have to look like an escapee from a travelling circus?

I made a face at Alice, and she made one back at me. But then I smiled. I was going to summer camp for three whole weeks, and nothing else mattered – not even the fact that my parents are the least cool people in the history of the universe.

* * *

Half an hour later, the bus pulled away from the bus station. Dad and Rosie waved madly. Mum waved too, but I could see that she was crying. I felt kind of embarrassed, and sorry for her at the same time. Then I thought about the great time Alice and I were going to have, and I didn't think about how Mum felt any more.

I still couldn't understand how Mum had allowed me to go to camp. One afternoon, I'd just said, 'Mum, can I go to summer camp in Cork with Alice?' I tried to say it all casual-like – as if I hadn't been working up to it for days. As if I didn't expect her to list a hundred reasons why summer camp would be bad for me. And then Mum totally surprised me by saying, 'Of course you can, love.'

Maybe she was thinking about a crazy new plan for the vegetable garden. Or maybe her mind was gone fuzzy from eating too many sunflower seeds or something. I didn't care though – she had said 'yes' and that was all that mattered.

Anyway, that was all weeks ago. Now I was safely on the bus to camp. Mum and Dad and Rosie were getting further away every second. At last I was free.

For the first time that morning I allowed myself to relax. It was going to be a fantastic three weeks – I just knew it. Alice and I had read the camp website about a million times, and we knew everything there was to know. There were going to be all kinds of games and sports, and treasure trails and cook-outs and on the second last night, a huge disco. That was the thing I was looking forward to the most – I'd never been to a disco before. Even thinking about the disco made me feel all excited and jittery.

Alice and I settled into our seats on the bus. I

pulled the camp brochure from my bag, and read it for the thousandth time.

'Are we definitely going to do basketball as our main sport?' I asked.

(The camp offered four sports – basketball, tennis, hockey and soccer. Whichever one you picked was your 'main sport' and you spent three hours at it each morning.)

Alice nodded.

'Definitely,' she said. 'We agreed that ages ago. We both like it, and we'll be doing it in September at our new school, so it will be nice to have had some extra coaching. You haven't changed your mind, have you?'

'No way,' I said quickly. I've never played soccer or hockey, and I'm really bad at tennis, so I was glad that Alice wanted to do basketball too.

We read the brochure for a while, and then Alice said,

'Pity Grace and Louise weren't able to come in the end.'

I nodded, but I didn't really agree with her. I was kind of glad that by the time Grace and Louise decided that they wanted to come with us, there were no places left in the camp. Grace and Louise are both really nice, and they were very kind to me earlier in the year when Alice was still living in Dublin, but in a way I was looking forward to having Alice all to myself for three whole weeks. I felt like we deserved it.

We'd both had a rough year. First Alice's parents split up, and she had to move to Dublin for a while with her mother and her little brother Jamie. Then Alice lost it a bit, and came up with all these mad plans to get her parents back together. Anyway, that crazy stuff was all over now. Alice was back living in Limerick and the two of us were off to camp for three whole weeks of fun.

* * *

The journey to Cork took almost two hours, but it felt like about two minutes because Alice and I were chatting so much.

When we got off the bus, we were met by a man in a mini-bus, who drove us the last few miles to the camp, which was in a boarding school in a village a few miles outside the city. I wondered why Alice and I were the only ones on the bus, but was too shy to ask the driver.

We drove for about twenty minutes. Alice and I didn't talk – we were much too excited by now. At last we turned a corner, and I saw a set of huge iron gates, and a sign – *Newpark College*. We drove up the gravel drive, and little flutters of excitement started deep down in my tummy. I pressed my nose up against the window, and watched as we approached the huge old, ivy-covered building. I felt like a girl in a book, or a film. I felt like Harry Potter on his first day at Hogwarts, or Darrell on her first day at Malory Towers.

I felt as if my real life was beginning at last.

Chapter two

The mini-bus stopped at the front door. Alice and I climbed out, and took our rucksacks from the driver. There was no-one else around. The driver jumped back in to the bus, and was about to drive off, when Alice shouted to him.

'Hey, what are we supposed to do? Where are we supposed to go?'

He shrugged.

'I don't know, do I? I'm only the driver.'

'But where is everyone? There's supposed to be a camp on here.'

The bus driver shrugged again.

'Looks like you're the first ones here. Now I've got to go. I've got to pick up another lot at the railway station. I've got six more runs to do, and I really don't have time for hanging around chatting to you. Try finding Mrs Duggan, the camp leader. Follow the signs saying office.'

'OK, thanks,' called Alice, as he drove off with a big spray of gravel.

Alice picked up her rucksack and led the way in through the huge doors. I followed her. I was glad she was there. If I'd been on my own I'd probably have stood outside on my own like a big eejit, waiting for someone to come along and find me and tell me what to do.

We quickly found the office. Alice knocked loudly on the door.

'Come.' It was a deep, cross-sounding voice.

Alice and I looked at each other. That wasn't

the kind of voice that camp leaders on the television had.

This was all wrong.

Where were the happy, bouncy women in track-suits and the jolly men with silly voices?

Alice made a face at me, and then she opened the door and went inside. I followed her because I couldn't think of anything else to do.

Mrs Duggan sat behind a huge wooden desk. (We knew she was Mrs Duggan because she was wearing a big shiny badge with her name on it.) She was writing long lists of numbers into a huge book. She didn't look up.

Suddenly I felt a bit afraid, and a bit stupid.

Maybe Alice and I were meant to be somewhere else.

Maybe we were never meant to approach Mrs Duggan at all.

Maybe she was the kind of person you only got to see if you were in really, really bad trouble.

Was it too late to turn around and run out the

door, and pretend that we had never been there at all?

Alice gave a small cough. Mrs Duggan didn't even look up. She just kept concentrating on her book. I was beginning to wonder if she'd forgotten all about us, when she finally put down her pen, took off her glasses and looked at us fiercely.

'Well?'

I didn't say anything. I didn't have to, because I knew Alice would crack first. Sometimes it's nice being the quiet one in a friendship.

After a few seconds, Alice spoke softly.

'We're here for the summer camp.'

Mrs Duggan made a sudden snorting noise.

'Well, I hardly thought you were here to repair the roof.'

There was another long silence. Finally brave Alice spoke again.

'Where should we go? What should we do?'

Mrs Duggan gave a big long sigh, like we were

really annoying her just by existing.

'You're early. No one's meant to be here for another hour.'

'We got the bus.' Alice said this confidently, as if it explained everything.

Mrs Duggan sighed again.

'Names?'

'Alice O'Rourke and Megan Sheehan.' This was Alice again. I felt like my tongue had gone on strike.

Mrs Duggan picked up a sheet of paper and looked at it for a long time. Then she said in a cold voice.

'You're in room 28. Second floor. Your group leader will come and get you at tea-time. Now run along and don't bother me again.'

We left the room, and closed the door carefully behind us.

Alice giggled.

'I soooo do not want to meet her again. I'm going to be on my very, very best behaviour.'

I grinned.

'Me too.'

We both meant what we said, but I wasn't sure how things would turn out. Alice hadn't mentioned secret plans yet, but trouble seemed to have a funny way of following her around, whether she liked it or not.

It took us ages to find room 28. It was a bit creepy, wandering around the deserted school. If we spoke in anything louder than a whisper, our voices echoed loudly, like they were the first sounds heard in the building for hundreds of years.

As usual, Alice was much braver than me, opening doors, peeping into rooms, and racing around corridors. She even slid down a big curvy banister.

She laughed out loud as she got to the bottom, and then covered her mouth as her echoed laugh bounced madly around the huge space.

'That was sooooooooooooooo much fun,' she

whispered. 'Come on, Meg. You do it. I'll stand here and catch you if you go too fast.'

I shook my head. I was never as brave as Alice. And I really didn't want to find myself back in front of Mrs Duggan's desk again so soon.

'No thanks,' I said. 'We have to find our room. And I need to find a toilet.'

I didn't really need the toilet. I just said it to get Alice away from the banisters – otherwise she'd have slid down over and over again, until she was caught.

Alice muttered a bit, but she followed me as we continued our search. At last we found room 28. The door opened with a loud creak. There were three beds, with a name tag on each: Alice, Megan and Hazel.

Alice picked up Hazel's name tag, and twirled it around in her fingers.

'Hazel's a nice name, isn't it? I wonder what she'll be like? It'll be fun sharing with someone new, won't it?'

I kind of half-nodded. I wasn't really looking forward to meeting this Hazel person. I'd have liked it better if it had been just Alice and me together. I couldn't say that though.

We started to unpack. I had brought all my best stuff, but when it was laid out on the bed, it looked a bit old and faded. My mum believes that a girl only needs three or four outfits, and that each one should last for about a hundred years.

I looked across at Alice's bed. Her stuff looked so much newer and brighter than mine – like it had all come out of a real expensive clothes shop about five minutes earlier.

She saw me looking.

'Hey,' she said. 'It's the broken home thing again.'

She was kind of right. She'd always had more clothes than me, but since her parents split up, she had more than ever. Her mum and dad seemed to be having a competition to see who could buy her the most things. Alice had a huge wardrobe in each parent's house, and both were stuffed full of really cool clothes.

Alice came over and dumped all her tops on to my bed.

'For these two weeks, let's not have "your stuff" and "my stuff". Let's just share everything.'

I smiled at her.

'Thanks, Al.' I said. I knew that given the choice, I wouldn't end up wearing any of my own stuff, but that didn't matter. Alice had more than enough for both of us.

I picked up a gorgeous turquoise top.

'This is sooo nice,' I said. 'Where did you get it?'

'Dad brought it back from Spain last month. Do you want a loan of it?'

I didn't answer. I was too busy feeling the soft fabric, and looking at the tiny green and yellow stripes, and the weenchy flowers embroidered on the sleeves. It was the most beautiful top I had ever seen.

'Well?' Alice was grinning at me.

I didn't know if I'd dare to wear it, it was so beautiful.

'Maybe....'

Alice laughed.

'How about you wear it to the disco? It would be great with your white jeans.'

All of a sudden I could see myself at the disco. For the first time in my entire life, (well since my christening day anyway) I'd be the best-dressed girl around. I nodded and Alice laughed some more.

We piled everything into one big wardrobe and then we sat on our beds and waited for our room-mate to arrive.

Every time we heard the sound of the minibus wheels on the gravel, we raced to the window and looked out. We watched as groups of girls and boys got out. Alice kept saying stuff like, 'bet that's Hazel,' or 'I hope *that's* not her, she looks really boring.'

Then we'd wait, and listen as girls came along our corridor, passed our door, and found their rooms.

I started to hope that maybe Hazel wasn't coming at all.

Maybe she had cancelled at the last minute.

Maybe she'd got some disease, not too serious, just bad enough to keep her away from summer camp.

Maybe it would be just Alice and me together in the room after all.

I'd have liked that.

* * *

Much, much later our bedroom door opened, and a girl walked in. She was really pretty, with curly blonde hair, and big brown eyes. She was wearing the coolest denim jacket I'd ever seen — with frayed cuffs and loads of studs and patches. My old rain jacket was on the bed next to me, and

I moved it under my blanket so it couldn't be seen.

The girl smiled, showing perfect white teeth.

'I'm Hazel,' she said.

Alice stood up.

'Hi, Hazel. I'm Alice, and this is Megan.'

We all said 'hi' and then there was a silence. I hate silences like that. I wished Hazel would just go away so Alice and I could get on with chatting.

I'd only known her for a minute, but already I didn't much like Hazel. She was a bit too confident – a bit too much like the kind of girl who liked to be in charge. Still though, I decided I was going to make a big effort to be nice to her. She wasn't as lucky as me – she hadn't got to go to camp with her very best friend in the whole world.

Chapter three

Hazel had a huge suitcase, and it seemed to take forever for her to unpack. Like Alice, she had heaps of fantastic clothes. I felt a bit like Cinderella with all my old raggy stuff. I felt sicker and sicker as she dragged more and more beautiful clothes from her case.

After a while she pulled out a totally cool denim skirt. Alice jumped up and touched it.

'That skirt is so nice,' she said.

Hazel shrugged.

'That old thing,' she said. 'That's so old I wasn't even going to bother bringing it.'

I started to laugh, before I realised that she wasn't joking. I made a face at Alice, but she didn't see me. She was too busy admiring Hazel's four new pairs of sports shoes.

At last Hazel seemed to be finished. She sat on her bed with a big sigh.

'I so hate unpacking,' she said. 'The only thing worse than unpacking is packing. I find it so hard to decide which clothes to bring. Don't you find that?'

'Yeah,' said Alice.

I didn't say anything. I didn't have any trouble choosing which clothes to bring. What would Hazel say if she realised that almost every piece of clothing I owned was stacked up in the wardrobe next to us?

Just then there was a knock on the door, and a

woman came in to our room.

'Hi, girls, I'm Gloria,' she said with the biggest smile I had ever seen. She had a huge mop of black curly hair, shiny black skin, and teeth that were whiter than the milk I'd poured on my porridge that morning.

She looked down a list that was pinned to a clipboard.

'You must be Alice, Hazel, and Megan.'

We all nodded.

Gloria continued.

'I'm your team leader for the week. If you have any questions, or any problems you all come to me. OK?'

We all nodded again.

Gloria didn't seem to mind that none of us appeared to be able to speak.

'Now all you second floor girls are in my group. Along with the boys from the ground floor. From now on you're known as the blue group. Got it?'

Once more the three of us nodded silently.

Gloria gave a big long laugh.

'Can't wait to hear your sweet voices,' she said. 'Tea is in five minutes. Go down the stairs and follow the signs for the dining hall. Last one down has to do all the washing up. It's camp tradition.'

Then she went out, half-closing the door behind her. There was a huge scramble as Alice, Hazel and I jumped up and raced to put on our shoes. Gloria put her head around the door, and treated us to one of her huge smiles.

'Just kidding. See you in five.'

* * *

Tea was great. Chips and sausages and heaps of ketchup – with nothing organic or healthy in sight.

All the blue group had to sit in one section of the dining room. There were also sections for the red, yellow and green groups. I sat with Alice of course, and she invited Hazel to sit with us.

Hazel barely stopped talking. She told us all about her big house and her pony and how she was going to America for four weeks as soon as camp was over. She went on so much about her fabulous life that she almost put me off my sausages. By the time tea was over, I was really fed up of her, but Alice didn't seem to mind.

Gloria moved around all the blue tables, talking to everyone. When she came over to us, Alice said,

'Gloria, can I ask you something?'

Gloria smiled.

'Sure. Ask me anything.'

Alice hesitated.

'Well, it's about Mrs Duggan. Does she…? I mean is she ……'

Gloria laughed.

'Mrs Duggan is the big boss. You don't bother her. She won't bother you. If you've got a problem, you just come to me. OK?'

We all nodded. I was very relieved. There was

something really scary about Mrs Duggan, and if I never saw her again, it would have been too soon.

When we had finished eating, it was time to sign up for our optional sport. As Alice and I walked over to the notice board, Hazel followed us. She spoke in a loud voice,

'I'm doing tennis, that's for sure. I'm going to be playing a lot in America – after all, we will be staying in a place with eight tennis courts – so I need to get some practice in.'

Yessss. I thought. At least Alice and I would have a few hours a day away from her.

Suddenly Alice stopped walking. She looked at me.

'Maybe we should change to tennis too,' she said.

I couldn't believe what I was hearing.

'But we're doing basketball. We agreed. Remember?'

Alice shrugged.

'We do basketball at school all the time. Tennis will be fun. Let's change.'

'But I don't even like tennis,' I said. That was only half true. I don't mind it so much, but I'm really, really bad at it.

Alice shook my arm.

'Come on, Meg. Don't be so boring. Let's change to tennis.'

Hazel was watching us with her arms folded. She smiled sweetly at me.

'If you want to play basketball so badly, why don't you just sign up for it?' she said. 'And Alice can do tennis with me.'

I felt like crying.

Alice and I *always* do the same stuff.

We like the same stuff.

I opened my mouth, but no words came out.

Hazel went on.

'Or are you afraid to do anything without your best friend?'

I looked at Alice. She looked back at me, and

gave an embarrassed kind of smile. Hazel grabbed the pen that was tied to the notice board with a dirty piece of string. She found the tennis list and wrote her name in big roundy letters with a long swirl on the last letter. Trust her to have a fancy signature.

She handed the pen to Alice. Alice looked at me. I shrugged. I didn't know what to say. I wanted her to do basketball with me, but I didn't want to sound like a baby who depended on her for everything.

Alice looked at Hazel, and then back at me. Then she wrote her name on the tennis list. She handed me the pen.

'Tennis will be fun,' she said. 'Bet you'll love it.'

I stood there with the pen in my hand. I didn't know what to do. I'm so, so bad at tennis it's unbelievable. After five minutes on the court everyone would surely be laughing at me and wondering where such a loser had come from. Alice is a good tennis player, and Hazel probably had her own tennis court in the back garden, and was brilliant. I'd look totally stupid next to the two of them.

And I'm not too bad at basketball.

And Hazel's remark about being afraid to do anything without Alice hurt – probably because it was true.

My hand was actually shaking from the stress of trying to decide what to do. And then two girls behind me told me to hurry up, because they wanted the pen this year if possible. And so, I took a deep breath and reached over to the basketball list and wrote my name in small, shaky letters.

Hazel gave a smile of triumph.

'Good decision, Megan,' she said. 'If you're not totally brilliant at sport, it's probably best not to go for the tennis.'

Alice gave me a funny look. Then she smiled and said,

'We'll be together for all the rest of the time

anyway. It's no biggie.'

We set off, back upstairs to our bedroom. Hazel tucked her arm into Alice's, like she owned her. Alice kindly put her other arm in mine, and we walked like that, as if the three of us were stuck together. I felt a bit stupid. Alice and I don't usually do that arm-in-arm stuff.

Up in the bedroom, Alice and Hazel swapped iPods. Of course Hazel had a super-duper video one with a sparkly cover and about a million songs downloaded on to it. I had an ancient Walkman at the end of my rucksack, but there was no way I was taking it out. I knew Hazel would only laugh at it. So I sat on my bed and tried not to feel like a total loser.

After a while, Alice noticed that I was sitting on my bed looking cross. She came and sat next to me, and gave me one piece of her earphones, and we each half-listened to Hazel's cool songs.

All of a sudden I had a funny feeling that

summer camp was going to be a bit more complicated than I had expected.

Chapter four

After breakfast the next morning (not a single bowl of porridge in sight), we went up to our room to get ready for our activities. Alice and I were already in our track-suits, so we only had to clean our teeth and brush our hair. Alice had a big  box of new hair-slides, and she lent me a really nice blue one. She tied my hair up, and then twisted it around and tied it with the slide so it looked great. After that, I helped her to plait her hair. Then we sat on our beds and waited for Hazel.

Hazel had gone to breakfast in her tracksuit, but now she wanted to change. She spent ages deciding which of her many designer tennis dresses to wear. She tried each one on, and walked up and down the room like a model, asking Alice and me to decide for her. I knew she was just showing off, but I had to admit that she looked really lovely in each dress. Actually, she was so pretty she would have looked lovely in anything. Even my faded old tracksuit.

At last she was ready, and we all stood up to go. Alice hadn't brought a tennis racquet, but guess what? Hazel had two and was more than happy to lend one to her new best friend. As we went downstairs, Hazel walked next to Alice, telling her how 'super-great' it was that they were going to play tennis together. I wanted to laugh at Hazel, but I had no-one to laugh with, so I didn't bother.

Outside, Alice and Hazel had to go one way to the tennis courts and I set off the other way to the big sports hall for the basketball. I felt kind of lost and lonely – I hate doing stuff on my own.

Alice ran after me.

'I feel bad, Meg,' she said. 'I wish you were doing tennis too. Why don't you change to our group? No-one will mind, and someone will lend you a racquet.'

I was really, really tempted, but I knew it would have been a mistake. I'd heard Gloria telling one of the boys that after the first half-hour the tennis people would be divided into groups according to how well they could play. I knew for sure that I'd end up with the total beginners, and wouldn't be anywhere near Alice. And I didn't want to give Hazel any more reason to laugh at me. And so I was brave. I shrugged, and said, 'thanks, but no thanks,' and set off for my basketball session.

*　　*　　*

The basketball was really good. The two coaches

were nice. We did loads of exercises and drills first, and then we played some matches. I played my very best, and was put on a very good team. There was a really funny boy called Sam on my team. He was the best player there by miles, but he wasn't all conceited and horrible. He messed around a lot, and made us all laugh with his jokes. One of the girls on my team, Sarah, was really nice too, and she asked me to sit with her and her friends when we took a break for juice and biscuits. And the biscuits were chocolate ones, and we could eat as many as we liked.

So I should have been really happy.

But I wasn't.

I kept on thinking of Alice and Hazel together. Hazel would be laughing at Alice's jokes, and Alice would be admiring Hazel's tennis shots. At break-time they'd be sitting together, having such a great time, and not thinking of me at all.

Everyone had lunch together. The tennis

people were back late, so when I came out of the queue with my tray, I didn't know where to sit. Sam was there with some of his friends, but I was too shy to go over and join them.

Then Sarah saw me and called me over. I sat down with her, and we ate and chatted for a while. I couldn't really concentrate on what Sarah was saying though, because I kept watching the door for Alice to come in. It was totally pathetic, I know. But I couldn't help it.

After about twenty minutes, the tennis group came in. They were all laughing and breathless. At the end of the group, Alice and Hazel were together. Hazel had her arm around Alice's shoulders, and Alice didn't even look embarrassed. This made me really cross, because Alice and I used always laugh at Melissa (the meanest girl in our school) when she and her friends went around like that.

I waved, and Alice and Hazel came over and joined us as soon as they had picked up their food. They went on and on and on about their totally cool tennis coach, and how good-looking he was, and how he once played in Wimbledon, and how he had this special technique for teaching how to serve and how everyone had improved so much already. In the end I felt like throwing up all over my jelly and custard.

After lunch we had art and French and then we went orienteering. Alice and I did everything together, as usual. This was different to usual though, because every time I turned around, Hazel was there beside us, bragging about something.

In some ways, Hazel reminded me of Melissa – always boasting – always trying to be the centre of attention. The big difference was, Alice had always hated Melissa, but she seemed to love Hazel.

Why couldn't she see through her?

Why couldn't she see what she was really like?

What was going on?

As the afternoon went on, Alice must have noticed that I was feeling a bit jealous. She was really nice, and she was careful not to pay too much attention to Hazel, and she didn't mention tennis once. It didn't help though. With every minute that passed, I found myself hating Hazel even more.

In art class I kept hoping that Hazel would get tangled up in the pottery wheel until she was all wrapped around it like a big long smiley snake.

In French I kept hoping that she would be so bad at grammar that the teacher would send her to Mrs Duggan's office for the day.

And in orienteering, I kept hoping that she'd take a wrong path in the woods, and never be seen again.

I know this all makes me seem really, really mean. But I couldn't help it – honest. You see Alice had been my best friend since we were toddlers. And in the past year when she'd been having such a hard time, I'd always been there for her. Whenever Alice got a crazy notion, I was there, waiting to help her. And I didn't mind. That's what friends do, isn't it?

And at Easter, when Alice finally got her greatest wish, and came back to live in Limerick, I was there waiting for her. I'd never given up on her. Ever.

The way I saw it was this – there were a hundred girls and boys in the camp, and Hazel could have had any one of those for her best friend.

Any one at all.

As long as it wasn't Alice.

I only wanted Alice.

Chapter five

On the second morning, I woke up slowly. I opened my eyes and looked around the unfamiliar room. Then I smiled. It wasn't a dream. I really was at summer camp.

Then I looked over and saw Hazel, and my smile faded. She was still asleep, with her curly blonde hair spread out on the pillow, like she'd spent hours arranging it. I made a face. So it wasn't a nightmare. She really did exist.

Alice and Hazel were soon awake. We all got up and got dressed slowly. I picked my track-suit bottoms off the floor, and looked at them. They seemed even older and shabbier than they had the day before. I sighed as I pulled them on. I knew Alice would have lent me some of hers, but I was taller than her now, and I knew they'd have been too short.

Alice must have seen my look.

'Here,' she said, as she reached into the wardrobe. 'Why don't you wear this t-shirt?'

I smiled at her and took it. Maybe if I wore that, no-one would notice how old my track-suit bottoms were.

This morning it only took Hazel ten minutes to decide which tennis dress to wear. Then she decided that Alice should be wearing a dress too. I knew Alice would prefer to play in shorts, or a track-suit, like she usually did, but somehow she ended up in one of Hazel's dresses. It looked really great on her.

By this time, I was bored of talking about tennis dresses, and ready to go down to breakfast.

'Come on, guys,' I said. 'Let's get going.'

Hazel gave me one of her lazy looks.

'You go if you want, Megan. I'm not ready yet.'

I sighed. This girl was really starting to annoy me. She looked ready to me. Her hair was tied up in a clever twisty kind of knot, her dress was buttoned up, and her snow-white tennis shoes were carefully laced. What else was there to do?

Hazel reached into a drawer next to her bed, and pulled out a large pouch.

'I haven't done my make-up yet. I didn't have time to do it yesterday, and all day I felt wrong without it.'

I started to snigger, and looked over at Alice. She wasn't sniggering though. She didn't act like Hazel was saying anything funny.

Hazel began to spread the contents of the pouch onto her bed. It was like a chemist's shop, with about a hundred bottles and tubes and jars.

She picked up a small mirror, and did her face carefully.

When she was finished, she caught Alice by the arm.

'What kind of eye make-up do you like best?' she asked her.

I held my breath and waited for Alice's reply.

What would her new friend say when Alice told her what she thought of eye make-up?

Alice's answer came too quickly.

'Oh you know. Eye-shadow. Mascara. The usual stuff.'

Now I gasped. Why was Alice lying? Neither of us ever wore eye make-up. It was kind of like a pact between us. Sometimes we wore lip-gloss, but that was about it when it came to make-up. Wearing loads of make-up was one of the things Alice and I used to laugh at Melissa for.

I stared at Alice, but she didn't look at me. She was sitting on Hazel's bed, and examining a tube of something green and shiny, like it was the coolest thing she'd ever seen. What was going on here? The only time Alice ever had make-up was when she got something free on the front of a magazine, and usually when that happened she just dumped it in a drawer and never touched it again. (Except once when she was doing up my Aunt Linda's face, but that's a different story.)

By now the bed was covered with stuff. Hazel pulled Alice even closer.

'Sit there,' she said, 'and I'll do your eyes for you.'

Alice didn't argue. She just tilted her head back, and closed her eyes.

I felt like closing my eyes too. I so did not want to watch this.

What was Alice at?

Why was she going along with Hazel?

Why was she so keen to please her?

I pretended to be busy tidying my locker, and a few minutes later Hazel was finished. Alice stood up and went over to the mirror. Then she turned to me.

'What do you think?'

I didn't know what to say. Her eyes did look lovely. Kind of brighter, and bigger. But she didn't look like Alice any more.

'It's nice,' I said quickly.

Alice didn't seem to notice that I wasn't very enthusiastic.

'Do Megan now, Hazel,' she said.

Hazel looked at me. She didn't seem very pleased. Still, how did she think I felt?

'I'm sure Megan doesn't want her eyes done,' said Hazel.

'Of course she does,' argued Alice.

For one second I was glad that they were arguing, but then I remembered that it was my eyes they were arguing about, and I didn't feel so great.

'You don't want your eyes done, do you Megan?' said Hazel in a voice that was almost threatening.

She was right. I didn't want my eyes done, but I didn't want to sound stupid either. And I didn't want to find myself agreeing with Hazel, and going against Alice.

So I didn't resist when Alice pushed me down on to the bed. Hazel gave a sigh, like this was a total pain, and then she picked up a few bottles she hadn't used before, and did my eyes.

When she was finished, I went and looked in the mirror. Hazel hadn't been trying, and it showed. My little sister Rosie could have done better than that. My two eyes didn't even match. And one was kind of black, like someone had punched me.

Hazel stood up.

'Come on, let's go down to breakfast.'

I hesitated. I couldn't go down to breakfast with my eyes looking like that. Everyone in the camp would laugh at me.

Alice looked at me. She knew I felt stupid, but she didn't want to offend her new friend by saying that the make-up she'd put on me looked awful.

We all stood there for a minute. Hazel had a

real mean look on her face, like this whole thing had been a battle, and she'd won.

Then Alice leaned over and looked closely at my eyes.

'One of your eyes has gone a bit red, Meg,' she said. 'Maybe you're allergic to that eye make-up.'

I went and looked in the mirror. My eyes didn't look red. They looked green, and mauve, and black and pink. In fact they were very, very colourful. But they weren't red. I opened my mouth to say so, but Alice poked me in the ribs and made a face at me.

'Look closer. You'd better take it all off. Quick.'

At last I understood what was going on. She'd thought of a way of saving me from being mocked, but still she hadn't hurt Hazel's feelings. She handed me a nice-smelling wipe from Hazel's stash on the bed, and I wiped my eyes until I looked normal again, and then we all went down to breakfast.

I'd only been up for half an hour, and already I was exhausted.

Chapter six

The first week of camp went fairly quickly. In the mornings, I quickly put on one of my old tracksuits, and then watched while Alice and Hazel made a big fuss about choosing their tennis dresses.

Then I watched them while they put on their make-up. (After the morning when Hazel made a mess of my eyes, there was no way I was letting her near them again.)

After breakfast every morning, I played basketball, and hung out with Sarah and her friends, while Alice and Hazel skipped off to their tennis and fell more and more in love with their handsome coach.

In the afternoons and evenings, Hazel and I jostled to be near to Alice. Alice must have noticed, but she didn't say anything. She'd had a difficult year, with her parents splitting up, and all the moving around, so she probably just wanted an easy life.

One really warm morning, Sarah and I were really tired after basketball, so we lay down under a tree in the garden to rest for a while. Sarah was telling me a really funny story about a girl in her class, when we heard the sound of laughing. Sarah sat up and looked towards the sound. She sighed.

'Oh, it's just the tennis group, coming back from their "wonderful" tennis lessons.'

I sat up too. Alice and Hazel were surrounded by three other girls. They were so busy chatting and laughing, they didn't notice Sarah and me. I watched Alice. She was still giddy, and funny and daring – she was still the same girl I'd been friends with for most of my life.

And yet she wasn't.

With her make-up, and with her hair tied up a cool new way, and in Hazel's tennis dress, suddenly she didn't seem like my friend any more.

Was she turning into one of the 'popular' girls?

Had Alice turned into one of the girls who wouldn't want someone like me hanging around with her?

'Hello?' said Sarah. 'Have you heard a single word I've been saying?'

I could feel my face going red.

'Sorry,' I said. 'I was thinking of something else. What did you say again?'

Sarah shook her head.

'It doesn't matter.'

Now I felt really bad.

'I'm sorry,' I said. 'Tell me again.'

Sarah smiled at me.

'It's OK, honestly.' She hesitated, and then said, 'You and Alice have been friends for a long time, haven't you?'

I nodded, and then Sarah continued.

'So you must really hate the way Hazel is trying to push you out.'

I didn't say anything. I picked a long piece of grass and wrapped it around my finger. So I wasn't imagining it. Even Sarah, who hardly knew us, could see that Hazel was being really mean to me.

'You can tell me if you like,' said Sarah. 'I'm a good listener.'

For a second I was tempted. It would have been nice to tell someone how I felt. Just then Alice saw us.

'Hi Megan. Hi Sarah,' she called. 'How was basketball?'

She ran over and threw herself onto the grass beside us. Hazel looked like she was going to follow her, then she changed her mind.

'Hey, Alice,' she called. 'Aren't you going to come and get changed?'

'In a minute,' called Alice.

'I have this really cool t-shirt upstairs. I'll lend it to you if you like.'

Alice started to stand up.

'Sorry, I've got to ......' she started to say to me, before Sarah interrupted her.

'Tell us again about your tennis coaches,' she said. 'I think the one with the dark hair is really cute.'

I could see that Alice didn't know what to do. She really wanted to follow Hazel, but she didn't want to be rude to Sarah. After a minute she sat down again.

'You go ahead,' she called to Hazel. 'I'll be there in a while.'

Hazel tossed her curly hair and stamped off towards the school.

I smiled at Sarah, trying to thank her, and she smiled back.

Chapter seven

Soon it was Sunday, the only day of the week when normal camp activities stopped. That meant no basketball for me and no tennis for Alice and Hazel. In the morning we got to stay in bed for another hour, and for me there was the extra-special treat of not having to watch Alice and Hazel dancing around our bedroom in their tennis-dresses.

While we were on our way down to breakfast, Gloria appeared.

'I need some help with something,' she said.

'Alice, Hazel, can you give me a hand for a minute?'

'Sure,' they said together, and followed her back upstairs.

'I'll keep you both seats,' I said, as I continued down the stairs.

A few minutes later, Alice and Hazel joined me.

'What did Gloria want you for?' I asked.

Hazel made a face.

'None of your business.'

I looked at Alice who had gone red.

'Nothing really,' she said. 'Gloria just wanted us to help her with something. It's no big deal.'

If it was no big deal, why did Hazel look so cross? Just then Sarah and Sam and some of Sam's friends came and sat down next to us, and I forgot all about it.

As soon as breakfast was over, Gloria shushed everyone, and then made an announcement.

'Tonight is a very big night,' she said. 'Tonight you are all invited to a star-studded show in the big hall.'

There was a moment's silence and then lots of chatter. Sarah raised her hand.

'Who are the stars?' she asked.

Gloria smiled at her.

'I'm glad you asked me that,' she said. 'Because you are the stars.'

There was more excited chatter and then Gloria shushed us all again.

'It's a talent show. You can sing, dance, juggle, whatever.'

A boy I didn't know put up his hand.

'Do we all have to do something?'

Gloria nodded.

'Yes. It's an official camp activity so everyone takes part. No exceptions.'

I started to feel nervous. Mum always says that I have heaps of talents. Maybe she's right, but none of them is really suitable for a talent show. I couldn't go on stage and bake a chocolate cake, or show off my basketball dribbling skills, could I?

Another boy put his hand up.

'Do we have to be on our own?'

Gloria shook her head.

'No. Everyone will work with a partner.'

'Can we pick our partners?' a girl asked.

'Yes,' said Gloria. 'And as there's an even number of you, no-one will be left out. Now you have all day to practise, and the show is on at seven thirty. So pick your partners, and get practising.'

There was a flurry of activity as kids jumped up from their tables and grabbed their friends.

For me, time seemed to slow down. Alice looked at Hazel, and then looked at me. At the other side of the table, I could see that Sarah was already arm in arm with one of her school-friends. I didn't dare to say anything. If I couldn't be with Alice, I really didn't want to be in the show at all, but I knew Gloria would never allow that.

Still, I didn't want to ask Alice to be with me.

After she picked tennis with Hazel instead of

basketball with me, I was afraid.

What if she said no?

What if she picked Hazel again?

After what felt like hours, Alice turned to me again.

'You and me together, Meg?' she said.

I could have hugged her.

Why hadn't I trusted her?

She'd been my best friend since forever, so of course she would want to be my partner.

Then I nodded, like it was no big deal.

'Sure,' I said. 'Why not?'

I looked at Hazel, who had a funny expression on her face. Suddenly I felt sorry for her – even though she'd been mean to me. It must have been hard not having a best friend to rely on.

'What about you Hazel?' I asked. 'Who are you going to be with?'

Alice pointed to the other side of the room.

'Look over there, Hazel,' she said. 'There's lots of people over there who don't have partners yet.'

Hazel stood up.

'Yeah, all losers I suppose,' she said as she walked away. 'Now I'd better get over there or I'll be stuck with someone totally useless.'

Just then Gloria came over.

'Anyone who's got a partner, get out of here. Go find yourself a quiet spot and get practising.'

So Alice and I went outside to plan our big performance.

Alice had a great idea for an act where I was a patient and she was an incompetent doctor, who kept misunderstanding what was wrong with me. We both thought of heaps of great jokes, and we practised for ages. It was such fun.

As soon as we were happy with our act, we went to the basketball court and hung out with all the other kids who were finished their practice. There was no sign of Hazel. I felt really good. We were going to have a great night – I just knew it.

Chapter eight

After tea, everyone was nervous as we went into the big hall.

Alice and I were due onstage in the second section of the show, so in the beginning we sat in the audience, and watched the first few acts.

Sam and his friend went first. They were dressed up like girls and sang a pop song in high-pitched voices. They were really bad singers, but everyone was laughing so much, it didn't matter. After that two girls told jokes, and then a boy and a girl sang together. Next came Hazel and another girl, Lisa, singing a Michael Jackson song. During the chorus, Hazel did a proper moonwalk, and everyone clapped and cheered.

Next it was time for Alice and me to go backstage. As we waited to go on, my hands were shaking so much I could hardly hold the blanket I was supposed to lie under.

'I'm *so* nervous,' I whispered to Alice. 'I'm going to make a complete mess of our act. I just know it.'

Alice hugged me.

'Don't be silly. You were great this afternoon when we practised, and I know you're going to be great now. In fact, you're going to be fantastic.'

She sounded so sincere, I felt better, and even managed to smile at her as Gloria waved and called for us to go on stage.

I followed Alice onto the stage, blinking in the bright spotlights. I *so* wanted to be somewhere else. I took a deep breath, and lay down under my blanket, as Alice sat on the small stool she'd carried on with her.

Alice gave me a big wink.

'Well, what seems to be the trouble Mrs Wobblebottom?' she said.

The audience roared with laughter, and I knew everything was going to be OK.

When our act was finished, everyone clapped and screamed, and I knew that we'd been good.

'You were great,' said Alice as we ran off stage.

'So were you,' I said.

Then we hugged each other. For the first time since Hazel had come barging into our lives, I felt really happy.

Then we found our seats and watched the rest of the show.

*   *   *

When the show was over, we all went in to the dining hall for orange juice and biscuits. Every-one was excited. Some people were still in their stage clothes, and some were wearing crazy make-up. There were lots of shouts of 'You were great!' and 'You were so funny!' and 'I was *soooo* nervous at first!'

After a while, the dining hall got really hot, and I decided to go out into the garden for a while to cool off. I was walking around, letting the night air cool my face, when I heard a familiar voice from behind a tall hedge. It was Hazel. Now that I was having such a good time, I didn't hate her so much any more, and I wanted to tell her that her moonwalk had been really cool. Maybe she'd teach Alice and me how to do it.

I started to walk around the hedge when I heard another voice. It was Jordan, a boy from Alice and Hazel's tennis group. I took another few steps, and then stopped. Hazel was always going on about boys and boyfriends. Maybe she and Jordan weren't just chatting. Maybe this was like a date – and if it was a date, I *so* did not want to be part of it. Luckily they hadn't seen me, and I decided to sneak away before they did.

I was turning to go back inside when I heard

Jordan say,

'Your act was really good, Hazel. That moonwalk was fantastic.'

I stopped walking, and heard Hazel give a happy little sigh.

'Thanks, Jordan,' she said.

'And your friend Alice was great too. Really funny.'

'Yeah, Alice was the best – but what did you think of her loser friend Megan?' asked Hazel.

Loser?

How dare she call me a loser?

'Weeeell, I didn't really notice Megan,' said Jordan.

Hazel gave an evil laugh.

'How could you have noticed her? She just lay there on the stage and watched while Alice did all the funny stuff. That girl is such a total dork.'

I felt like stamping my foot. That was so not fair. I had lots of funny lines in our act, and I'd thought of most of them myself. I wished Alice was there to defend me. She'd never let Hazel say stuff like that about me.

I'd made up my mind to go back inside when Jordan spoke again.

'How come you weren't with Alice in the talent show anyway? Aren't you two best friends?'

Hazel gave a funny giggle.

'Totally. Alice and I, we're, like, you know, soul mates.'

Soul mates?

If I hadn't been so cross, I'd have thrown up.

'So why weren't you and Alice together?' repeated Jordan.

Hazel gave a big long sigh.

'We would have been together. We do everything together these days, but that horrible Gloria told Alice this morning that she had to go with Loser-Megan. So we had no choice. Otherwise Alice would definitely have been with me. She said so.'

I gasped.

Hazel had to be making this up.

Didn't she?

But Gloria *had* spoken to Alice and Hazel earlier.

But I thought she'd asked them to help her with something?

I tried to think properly, but I couldn't. My mind was all mixed up. At the other side of the hedge I could hear Jordan and Hazel laughing at something – probably me.

I didn't want to hear any more. I ran back inside and found Alice. She was chatting to Sam and some of the other boys.

I grabbed her arm.

'I need to talk to you. Urgently,' I said.

Alice laughed.

'Yeah, right.'

I squeezed her arm.

'I'm not joking,' I hissed. 'I really need to talk to you.'

Alice laughed again.

'Whatever,' she said.

'Sorry,' I said to Sam and the others. 'She'll be right back.'

Alice was laughing, and acting normally. Everything had to be all right. Didn't it?

I found a quiet spot at the end of the stairs.

'Well,' said Alice. 'What's so urgent?'

I hesitated. I wanted to know the truth, and yet I didn't.

'Hello? Earth calling Megan,' said Alice. 'If we don't go back inside soon, all the nice biscuits will be gone.'

How could she think of biscuits at a time like this?

'It's about the show,' I said quickly.

Alice looked puzzled.

'What could be so urgent about the show? It was great, and now it's over.'

I took a deep breath.

'Why did you ask me to be your partner?'

'Because you're my friend,' said Alice quickly.

Half of me wanted to leave it at that, but the other half had to keep going.

'Is that the only reason?'

Alice hesitated.

'Weeeeell, you see …… ' she started to say, and then I knew the truth.

'Gloria said you had to go with me, didn't she?' I said quietly.

'How do you ……?' asked Alice.

Now I knew for sure.

'Don't worry about how I know,' I said, 'just tell me what happened.'

Alice spoke very softly.

'It was nothing really. Let's forget about it.'

Now I really did stamp my foot.

'I can't forget about it. Tell me what happened.'

Alice sighed.

'OK. This morning when Gloria asked me and Hazel to help her, she didn't really need our help. She just told us about the talent show. And then she……'

'And then she what?'

'And then she said I was to be with you.'

'Why?'

Alice hesitated again.

'She said something about not leaving you out. She said—'

Suddenly I didn't want to hear any more. I put up my hand to stop Alice talking. We stood there, staring at each other. So Hazel had been telling the truth. Alice only picked me because she had to. I could feel tears coming to my eyes, and I *so* did not want Alice to see me crying.

'I'm going to bed,' I said, turning away.

Alice grabbed my arm.

'Don't go,' she said. 'Come back in to the dining hall with me. Everyone's there having fun.'

I tried to pull free, but Alice wouldn't let go of my arm.

'Megan,' she said.

'What?'

'I would have picked you anyway.'

But she didn't meet my eyes when she said this, and I knew for sure that she was lying.

I gave a sudden tug, and pulled free of her grip. Then I ran upstairs, threw myself onto my bed and cried myself to sleep.

Chapter nine

In the morning I woke up to the sound of Hazel rummaging through her wardrobe. She was sighing loudly. 'I just can't decide what to  wear this morning,' she said.

I looked over towards Alice's bed. Alice was looking at me. She smiled.

'Hi, Meg,' she said. 'You should have come back to the party with me last night. It was great fun.'

I felt like screaming at her. Didn't she know? It was all her fault that I didn't go to the party. So why did she care so much now?

But I was tired, and I had a headache, and I

didn't feel like a row, especially not in front of Hazel, so I didn't say anything.

Alice was really nice to me that day. She lent me her new hoodie, and at breakfast she gave me the last of her precious chocolate cereal. At lunch time, she chatted much more to me than she did to Hazel, and when bed-time came around, I'd decided that the whole talent show thing was no big deal, and I made up my mind to forget all about it.

The next few days were kind of strange. Hazel kept following Alice and me around, like some kind of lost puppy-dog. She wasn't especially mean to me, but she wasn't nice either. And I couldn't forgive her for telling Jordan that I was a loser. So when the three of us were together, Hazel and I both talked to Alice, but ignored each other, while Alice did her best to talk to both of us, and act like there was nothing strange going on.

In a way it was a relief when Alice and Hazel

went to tennis, and I could relax with Sarah and Sam and the others in my basketball group.

One morning I was walking back from basketball with Sarah, when she said,

'What's going on between you, Alice and Hazel these days?'

I sighed.

'I don't know really. It's all totally weird.'

Sarah hesitated.

'Want to know what I think?'

I nodded.

'I think Hazel is a total bully. She doesn't just want to hang out with Alice – it's like she wants to own her. And she hates you because you're the one that Alice likes the most.'

I gave a small smile.

'Thanks. I used to think that Alice liked me the most, but now I'm not sure any more. It's like Hazel is so strong that she's trying to take over Alice's mind. Alice is different here. It's like Hazel has made her become a different person.

Does that sound crazy?'

Sarah laughed.

'Not a bit.'

'So what should I do?'

Sarah thought for a moment.

'Don't do anything. Alice is your best friend. Trust her to do the right thing.'

I sighed. She was probably right.

* * *

At lunch-time, I sat with Alice and Hazel. It was OK at first, and then Hazel started to talk about Jordan. (I'd been right about them being on a date the night after the show.) Every sentence started with 'Jordan says' or 'Jordan thinks.' And the worst part was, Alice didn't even see the funny side of it. She acted like she really cared what Jordan says and thinks.

After a while Hazel ran out of things to say about Jordan.

'What about you guys,' she said. 'Have you had many boyfriends?'

I waited for Alice to answer – to tell her that we weren't really into boys. Hazel would probably feel a bit stupid for going on so much about Jordan, once she realised that Alice and I weren't ready for that kind of stuff yet.

I waited – and waited. And then I waited some more.

At last Alice answered.

'Well, I've only had a few boyfriends so far,' she said.

I started to laugh before I realised she wasn't trying to be funny.

What boyfriends had Alice had?

If she'd had even one, I'd know about it.

Wouldn't I?

Suddenly I understood that since Hazel had barged into our lives, I couldn't be sure of anything as far as Alice was concerned.

'The only one I really liked was Eliot,' continued Alice. 'He was really cool.'

Eliot?

What was she on about?

'Who's Eliot?' I blurted out without thinking.

'Oh, he was a guy who lived near us when I was in Dublin,' said Alice. 'We went out a few times.'

'But you never told me.' As soon as the words were out, I knew they made me sound like an idiot.

Hazel saw her opportunity. She put on a baby-voice.

'Aaaaw. Didn't Alice tell little Megan every single thing about her life? Poor little Megan.'

I waited for Alice to defend me, like she always did when Melissa used to pick on me at school. This time she didn't though. She just tossed her head.

'Oh, didn't I tell you that? Must have forgotten. It's no big deal anyway.'

I knew my face was going red. I felt so stupid.

Was Alice making up this whole Eliot thing?

Or had she really had this whole relationship

that I knew nothing about?

Hazel gave me an evil smile, then she turned to Alice.

'Don't worry about it. Looks like Megan's never had a boyfriend. So why would you discuss that kind of stuff with her? Why don't you and I go for a walk? I want to hear every detail about Eliot – every single detail.'

She got up, and left the table. Alice stood up too. I wanted to make a face at Alice, to let her know … well I don't know what I wanted to let her know. It didn't matter anyway, because Alice didn't even look back at me as she followed her new best friend outside.

Chapter ten

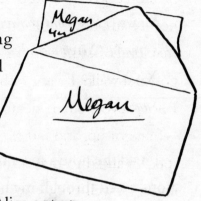

The next morning started the usual way. Hazel was up first planning her clothes and make-up for the day.

Ten minutes later, Alice got up and picked up her towel.

'I'm going for a shower,' she said. 'See you guys in— what's this?'

As she said the last words she bent and picked up an envelope that was half under our bedroom door. She turned it over, and then handed it to me.

The front of the envelope said 'Megan' in small, neat handwriting.

I took it from her and opened it quickly. Inside was a small sheet of paper, with just a few words on it.

Megan. How 'bout you and I get together. After tea this evening? Seven o'clock at the basketball court?

XXX

Sam

I read the note a few times. All kinds of questions raced through my head.

What did those three xxx's mean?

Was Sam asking me on a date?

I liked Sam, but did I want him for a boyfriend?

Did I want anyone for a boyfriend?

Hazel and Alice were staring at me?

'What's the letter about?' asked Hazel, like she really cared.

I folded up the paper and stuffed it back into the envelope.

'Nothing really. It's——' I began, but stopped when Hazel grabbed the envelope from my hand, pulled out the page and read it aloud.

I waited for the laughing to begin, but to my surprise, Hazel didn't seem to think it was funny. She actually seemed impressed.

'So Sam's asking you out? He's the guy from your basketball group, isn't he?'

I nodded.

'He's kind of cute,' she said. 'You should go out with him.'

I didn't say anything.

Suddenly Hazel was being almost nice to me.

Even if I didn't really want a boyfriend yet, maybe it would be worth going out with Sam, just so Hazel would continue to be kind to me?

Maybe she'd even stop picking on me?

And if Alice had a boyfriend in Dublin that I'd only just heard about, maybe it was time for me to do some catching up?

And Hazel was right – Sam *was* kind of cute.

Maybe this was the best thing that could possibly have happened?

I looked at Alice.

'What do you think?' I asked. 'Should I go out with Sam?'

She didn't answer for a minute, then she spoke in a rush.

'I don't know. Whatever. Do whatever you want. Now I'm going for my shower.'

I was a bit upset that Alice didn't seem more enthusiastic, but it didn't matter. I'd made up my mind. I was going to live a little. I was going to meet Sam. And no-one was going to make me change my mind.

* * *

It was a bit embarrassing when I met Sam at basketball later, but he acted like everything was the same as usual. That seemed strange, but I decided he didn't want his friends to know about us in case they'd tease him. So I decided to act normally too.

Seems like I'm not very good at acting normally though, because as soon as she got the chance, Sarah pulled me into a quiet corner.

'What's with you this morning?' she asked.

I shrugged.

'I don't know what you're talking about.'

Sarah laughed.

'Don't bother lying,' she said. 'I know there's something going on. Every time Sam comes within five metres of you, you go all red and start fixing your hair.'

I gave a small smile, and it was enough to make Sarah jump up and down.

'I knew it,' she said. 'I just knew it. Now tell me everything. I want to know every single detail.'

I sighed.

'OK. But there aren't all that many details … yet.'

Sarah giggled, and then I continued.

'Sam's asked me to meet him after tea this evening. You know … like for a date. But don't tell anyone else – I don't think he wants his friends to know about it.'

Sarah giggled again.

'That's so cool. Sam is really nice. You might think this is stupid, but I … I … well I haven't had a boyfriend yet.'

I smiled at her.

'It's not stupid. I've never been on a date before either. Tonight's going to be my first.'

'Are you nervous?'

I nodded. I was really, really nervous. But I wasn't backing out – no way.

Chapter eleven

As soon as tea was over, I raced upstairs to get ready. Hazel and Alice followed me.

'I'll do your face for you,' offered Hazel.

I didn't answer. After the morning when she made my eyes look really weird, I wasn't sure that I could trust her.

Hazel smiled at me.

'That last time I did your eyes, I was kind of in a rush. I know I didn't do a very good job. I'll be more careful this time – I promise.'

'OK,' I said, and sat obediently while she did my face for me. When she was finished she held up a mirror so I could see what she had done. I had to smile – she'd almost managed to make me look pretty.

'Thanks, Hazel,' I said. 'Look, Alice. What do you think? Will Sam be impressed?'

Alice was playing with her phone.

'I suppose,' she said.

I wondered why Alice was acting so bored, but was interrupted when Hazel said,

'Now clothes. Would you like to borrow my jeans, and one of my t-shirts?'

I had kind of planned to ask Alice for a loan of her turquoise top, but since Hazel was being so friendly, I decided to wear her stuff.

I put on her jeans, and Hazel picked out two t-shirts. I held them up.

'Which one do you think is nicest?' I asked Alice.

Alice slowly looked up.

'Whichever,' she said, and looked back at her phone again.

I was starting to feel a bit hurt.

Why wasn't she interested?

Suddenly I had a horrible thought.

Was she jealous?

Was my best friend jealous because I was going on a date and she wasn't?

Again, I didn't have too much time to think about this, as Hazel was coming towards me with Alice's hair-straighteners, and a selection of ribbons and clips.

Five minutes later I was ready to go. Hazel practically pushed me out the door.

'You mustn't be late. Have a nice time.'

'OK,' I said, trying not to let her see how nervous I was. 'Bye, Hazel. Bye, Alice.'

Alice looked up again.

'Megan,' she said.

I turned back.

'What?'

She hesitated.

'... er ...... see you later.'

I walked slowly downstairs, and suddenly I didn't feel nervous any more

I was going on my first date.

How exciting was this?

* * *

It was just a minute after seven when I got to the basketball court. There was no-one there – not even Sam.

I sighed. Why did the first boy I had ever dated in my whole life have to be late?

Time passed very slowly.

I leaned up against the railings for a while.

I walked around the basketball court seven times.

I threw a pebble in the air and caught it two hundred and thirty-three times.

And still Sam didn't show up.

What was going on?

Had he forgotten?

Had he changed his mind?

I was starting to feel a bit stupid hanging

around on my own, all dressed up in Hazel's clothes.

After ages and ages I heard a call.

'Megan, over here.'

I looked up. It was Sarah, running along the path, and waving at me.

'What are you doing here?' I hissed as she came close. 'I'm supposed to be on a date.'

Sarah stopped, caught her breath, and spoke.

'There's something I have to tell you.'

I knew at once that it wasn't going to be good news.

'Go on,' I said. 'I'm ready.' (Even though I wasn't.)

'It's about the date,' began Sarah. 'You see, I went up to your room to wish you good luck, but you must have left already. The door was open, and I could see Alice and Hazel inside. They hadn't noticed me, and, as you know, I can't stand Hazel, so I decided to go back downstairs. Just as I was walking away, though, I realised they were talking about you and Sam. Hazel was laughing, and Alice said something like – *I knew from the very beginning that there was something strange about this whole thing.'*

'What did she mean?' I asked.

'Well, I didn't know at first,' said Sarah, 'but since you're my friend, I felt it was my duty to find out, so I stayed and listened some more.'

'And?' I wanted to know, and yet I so didn't want to know.

'Well, I can't remember every single word, but basically, it sounds like Hazel set you up. She wrote the note and pretended it was from Sam.'

It took me a minute to work out what she was saying.

'So there was no date?'

Sarah shook her head.

'I'm sorry,' she said.

Suddenly I had a horrible thought.

'Was Alice in on it?' I asked.

Sarah thought before answering.

'That's the bit I'm not sure about. She definitely knew it was a set up by the time I got there, but I couldn't make out when exactly she discovered that.'

Suddenly I felt angrier than I ever had in my whole life. I started to run back towards the school.

Sarah ran after me.

'Where are you going?' she asked.

'To have this out with Alice. If it turns out she knew about this, I am never *ever* going to speak to her again.'

'Do you want me to come with you?'

I shook my head.

'Thanks, Sarah, but no. This is something I have to do by myself.'

Then I went inside to pick a fight with my best friend.

Chapter twelve

By the time I got as far as my bed-room, I was so cross that I half-expected to feel smoke pouring out from my ears.

Alice was coming through the door.

'I was just coming to find you,' she said.

I pushed past her into the room. She followed me inside, and sat on her bed. Hazel was standing at the mirror, doing her hair as usual.

'Nice date?' Hazel asked, grinning.

I felt like grabbing her hairbrush and smashing it into her pretty, horrible face. I put my hands behind my back, suddenly afraid that I was actually going to do that.

I stamped over to where Alice was sitting. She was looking at me almost like she was afraid. The letter I had thought was from Sam was on the dresser next to her. Alice and Hazel must have been laughing together about it. I picked it up.

'What do you know about this?' I shouted.

'About what?' she said, like I wasn't actually waving it in front of her face.

'About this stupid, stupid letter that Hazel wrote, pretending it was from Sam.'

Now Alice looked really afraid.

'But how ... how do you know?'

I crumpled up the letter and threw it across the room.

'It doesn't matter how I know. I just know. Now tell me, what do you know about it?'

Alice looked at me, then she looked at Hazel, and then she looked back at me again.

'I know it was a set-up,' she said quietly.

'But when did you discover this?' I asked.

'Just a few minutes ago.'

Suddenly I didn't feel angry any more. I just felt all mixed up. I didn't know if I could believe her or not.

Hazel hadn't said anything yet. Now she spoke.

'Don't worry,' she said. 'It was all my idea. I told Alice after you had left for your "big date". I had to tell someone. It was just *so* funny. You were so excited about going on a date that was never going to happen.'

I wanted to think of something really clever to say, but I couldn't. All I could manage was,

'That was *so* mean, Hazel.'

Hazel shrugged.

'I don't know what all the fuss is about. It was just a bit of a laugh.'

'Well, I don't think it was very funny,' I said.

Now Hazel actually laughed.

'Well, maybe that's because you have zero sense of humour. Get over yourself, why don't you?'

I looked at Alice.

She was just sitting there watching us.

Why wasn't she helping me?

Hazel gave a big long sigh.

'I can't stand here chatting all evening. I'm going downstairs for the quiz. You coming, Alice?'

Alice stood up. I stared hard at her, trying to say *If you leave now, we're not friends any more,* without actually saying any words. She seemed to understand. She sat down again.

'You go on, Hazel,' she said. 'I'll be down in a minute. Keep a seat for me.'

Hazel went out, closing the door behind her.

I sat on my bed, folded my arms, and waited for Alice to say something. She didn't seem to be in much of a hurry. She was busy picking nail varnish off her thumb-nail.

Soon I couldn't wait any more.

'That was a really mean trick,' I said.

At last Alice looked up.

'I honestly didn't know about it until after you left.'

'So you had absolutely no idea?'

She hesitated.

'Well, I was a bit suspicious, this morning, when the note arrived. I had kind of a bad feeling about the whole thing.'

'So that's why you didn't help with my clothes and make-up?'

She nodded.

'But why didn't you say something?'

She shrugged.

'I don't know. I … well, Hazel was right.'

'What do you mean?'

Alice sighed.

'Look, I'm sorry you're so upset. Honestly I am. But you shouldn't take stuff so seriously. It's not such a big deal. It was just a bit of fun. Hazel didn't really mean to upset you.'

I could hardly believe my ears.

'Are you defending her?' I asked. 'Hazel did that *really* mean thing to me, and you're taking her side?'

After ages, Alice spoke again.

'Is this all because you're jealous of me and Hazel being friends?'

I didn't answer. I *was* jealous, but that wasn't the point.

'You're friends with Sarah, and I'm not making a big fuss about that, am I?' said Alice.

'But that's different,' I said.

'How?'

'Because … because … because Sarah doesn't try to own me. She hasn't changed me. I don't act like a different person when she's around. And she doesn't hate you just because you're my friend.'

'Hazel doesn't hate you,' said Alice. 'She's just a bit possessive. It's the way she is. She can't help it.'

Suddenly I was tired of arguing. I felt a bit better now that I knew Alice wasn't part of the date plot, but I still wasn't happy.

Alice stood up.

'I'm going downstairs,' she said. 'The quiz will

be starting soon. Are you coming?'

'Are you going to sit with Hazel?'

Alice nodded.

'You can sit with us too.'

I shook my head sadly.

Why couldn't Alice see the truth?

Why couldn't she see that Hazel was as mean as a snake?

Why couldn't she see that as long as Hazel was around, there was always going to be trouble?

'Come on down,' said Alice. 'It'll be fun. We can forget all this stupid date stuff, and have a bit of a laugh.'

But I knew I couldn't forget that easily, so I just shook my head, and Alice went out, closing the door behind her.

This was so, so unfair. I lay down on my bed and started to cry.

I was beginning to wish that I'd brought a waterproof pillow.

Much later there was a tap on my bedroom

door. It had to be Alice. I sat up and wiped my eyes.

'Come in,' I said.

The door opened and Sarah came in.

'Everything OK?' she asked.

I shook my head.

'Not really.'

Then I told her everything that had happened. She was really nice and understanding, even when I started to cry again.

She stroked my hair.

'Don't worry,' she said. 'Camp's more than half over. In a bit more than a week's time, Hazel will be far away from you and Alice, and everything will be OK again.'

I cried even more.

'This is summer camp,' I said. 'I'm supposed to be having the best time of my life. I'm not supposed to be wishing it was over.'

Sarah hugged me.

'I suppose you're right. Anyway, sit up, stop

crying and wipe your eyes. I haven't told you the best thing yet.'

I did what I was told, and Sarah started to giggle.

'It was the funniest thing ever,' she said.

'So tell me,'

'OK. Sam came over to me and asked where you were, and I told him—'

I grabbed her arm.

'You didn't tell him about the date?'

Sarah pretended to look cross.

'Do I look like a *total* idiot?'

I shook my head, giggling, and she continued,

'I just told him that you were upset because Hazel had played a really mean trick on you. And he seemed like he was really bothered by that. He said it was rotten to pick on you since you were so nice.'

'He really said that?'

Sarah nodded.

'Anyway, I didn't tell you the best bit yet. There

were glasses of Coke, and Sam went and got one and brought it over to Hazel, pretending to be really nice. And Hazel did that sweet smiley stuff she does around boys. And when she'd drunk the Coke, Sam gave her a big smile and said he hoped she enjoyed it because before he gave it to her, he and all his friends had spat in it.'

I put my hand over my mouth.

'I don't believe it.'

Sarah laughed.

'It was totally the funniest thing ever. You should have seen Hazel's face. She ran out to the toilets. Everyone could hear her washing out her mouth, and spitting, and crying. In seconds, we all knew what had happened. Soon, everyone was laughing at her.'

'Even Jordan?'

Sarah nodded.

'He looked like he was going to throw up, he was laughing so much.'

'And Alice?'

Sarah nodded again.

'Alice looked like she was trying not to laugh, but in the end she joined in with the rest of us.'

I was enjoying the picture of Hazel being mocked, when Sarah continued.

'No one really likes Hazel, you know.'

'No one except for Alice,' I corrected her.

'Well, we all have our weak points,' she said. 'Now, I'm going back downstairs for a while. Do you want to come?'

I shook my head.

'I think I'll just stay here and have an early night. But thanks, Sarah.'

She shrugged.

'No problem. That's what friends are for.'

Then she went out.

I lay down again.

Sarah was so, so nice.

She was everything you could want in a friend.

But she wasn't Alice.

Chapter thirteen

he next day, Alice was really nice to me again.

'Let's just go on as normal. Let's forget about yesterday,' she said. 'Let's act like it never happened.'

But how could I act like it never happened when every time I turned around, Hazel was there, making stupid jokes about dates and stuff?

And how could I go on as normal, when Hazel was doing her very best to come between Alice and me?

After basketball, Sam came over to me.

'Everything OK?' he asked.

'Sure,' I said, knowing that my face was turning red.

'I heard Hazel was mean to you last night. Do you want to tell me what she did?'

'No way,' I said so quickly that Sam jumped away as if I had hit him. 'I mean, no thanks,' I corrected myself. 'It was nothing really.'

'Sure?' asked Sam.

'Absolutely,' I said, thinking that I would die if Sam ever discovered what had happened.

Then I laughed.

'What you did to Hazel later on was brilliant. I can't believe you and your friends spat in her drink.'

Now Sam went red.

'Actually, we didn't,' he said. 'That would be totally gross. But she thinks we did, and that's all that matters.'

Now we both laughed together. It made sense in a way. I was upset over an imaginary date, and

Hazel was upset over imaginary spit in her drink.

'Got to go,' said Sam. 'But remember, if Hazel's mean to you again, just let me know, and I'll sort her out for you.'

'Thanks,' I said. No matter how bad things got, I couldn't see myself asking him for help, but it was really nice to know that he cared.

*　　*　　*

The next day was Sunday. This was visiting Sunday – the only day of the camp when parents were allowed to visit us, and to take us out for the day. Of course, Mum and Dad and Rosie were coming to visit me – Mum needed to check up on me, and make sure I was living the perfect, healthy life she expected of me.

Anyway after all the fights with Hazel and Alice, a quiet day out with my parents seemed just what I needed.

Alice's parents weren't visiting her. She had been clever – she had torn up her copy of the camp brochure, and then told them that visits weren't allowed.

'But what if they find out?' I'd asked. 'What if one of them talks to my parents and discovers the truth?'

Alice had shrugged.

'I'll just have to take a chance. Trust me, it's for the best,' she had told me. 'Mum and Dad are getting on a bit better nowadays, but they're hardly the best of friends. They'd never be able to agree which one of them should visit me, so it's best if no-one does.'

Poor Alice. At last she was kind of getting used to the idea of her parents not living together, but every time she talked about them, I could hear a strange kind of sadness in her voice. Once again I realised that, even though my parents are a total embarrassment, I should be grateful that they love each other.

I wondered if Hazel's parents were coming to see her. I was hoping they were. Maybe I'd get lucky. Maybe they'd take her far, far away and forget to bring her back.

During breakfast, I had to ask her.

'I'm not quite sure yet,' she replied. 'Mummy and Daddy are flying back from Dubai this morning. They might show up here, and then again they might not. My brother's staying with some friends in Cork, so they might visit him instead. It's cool anyway. I don't need them hanging around annoying me.'

When I heard this, I was very sorry that my family was coming. I still wanted to see them of course, but I couldn't bear to think that Alice and Hazel would get to spend the whole day together, without me. Hazel would have a whole day to tell Alice bad stuff about me, and I wouldn't even be there to defend myself.

Suddenly I had a crazy idea. Maybe I could phone home and say that there was an epidemic of something dreadfully contagious, and that all visits were now cancelled. Then I knew that would never work. Mum had probably been planning the trip since the day I left home. She'd probably knitted herself a new dress for the occasion. She'd have been soaking beans and stuff for at least three days, to make us a picnic lunch. If I told her that visits were cancelled, that wouldn't put her off. She'd drive here anyway, and climb up on the wall, and shout in at me, and throw packages of healthy food in my direction. Nothing could save me from her. I was doomed.

After breakfast, I went out to the garden with Alice and Hazel. It was a lovely day, so we lay on the grass and watched as the odd cloud drifted across the bright blue sky. After a while, Hazel made yet another joke about Sam, and the date that never happened.

'Give it a rest, Hazel,' said Alice, 'That is so not funny any more.'

I felt like jumping up and hugging her, but resisted. That would only have given Hazel another reason to mock me.

Shortly afterwards, Gloria came to tell me that

my family was outside waiting for me. Alice and Hazel walked around to the front of the school with me, even though I'd have preferred if they didn't.

Our car has four wheels, and an engine, and I'm glad of it when Dad drives me to school on wet days, but next to some of the very fancy cars in the driveway, it looked a bit old and battered. I was fairly sure that Hazel's parents drove a fancy jeep or something like that. Still, no point being too embarrassed about our car, since my delightful family was standing next to it.

Dad and Rosie looked sort of OK. (Well, maybe not OK, but not a total embarrassment either.) Mum though, was a different story. She looked a complete mess. I'm sure she had combed her hair some time in the past few weeks, but it didn't look like it. It was flying all over the place in the wind, like something designed to scare away birds. She was wearing baggy old faded trousers and a sleeveless top I knew she'd had since I was about six. (She'd probably had it since she was about six.) On her feet she had horrible clumpy brown sandals, and of course she hadn't discovered nail varnish in the weeks we'd been apart. And the worst of all was, when she raised her arm to wave at me, everyone could see that she doesn't believe in shaving, and her under-arm hair began to blow in the wind, in time with the hair on her head.

Aaaaargh.

As soon as they saw me, Mum and Dad ran over to me and hugged and kissed me.

Don't they watch TV?

Don't they know that kids my age *really* hate it when their parents kiss them in public?

Can't they remember what it was like to be young?

Or do they just do it out of spite – a little payback for all the times I dropped my clothes on the floor and left the bathroom tap dripping?

Rosie ran over to Alice who picked her up and

swung her around. Those two had always been great buddies. Luckily, even Hazel seemed to think that Rosie was cute. She tickled her, and gave her a sweet from her pocket. I giggled. Pity Mum didn't see that – if she had, she'd have tried to get Hazel expelled from the camp immediately, and all my troubles would have been over at once.

Dad looked at his watch.

'Come on you lot,' he said. 'It's a lovely sunny day, and I don't want to spend it here in the car park. Let's go.'

Mum looked at Alice.

'Are your parents coming to see you today?' she asked.

Alice shook her head.

'No. They'd like to, of course, but they're very busy.'

Mum didn't look very pleased to hear that. She was never too busy to give attention to Rosie and me. This was of course both a good and a bad thing – mostly bad.

Then she smiled at Alice.

'Maybe you'd like to come out with us for the day? You'd be very welcome, and I'm sure Megan would like to have you along.'

That was a totally brilliant idea. I could have kissed Mum, and right then I didn't care who was watching.

Alice looked a bit doubtful.

'Thanks,' she said. 'That's very nice of you, but...'

She stopped talking and looked at Hazel. I looked at Hazel too, and tried to make up my mind. Which would be worse – bringing Hazel and putting up with her for the day, or leaving her here with Alice?

If she came along with us, would she spend the last week of the camp mocking my mum's crazy ways, and my dad's so-not-funny jokes?

I had a pain in my head from trying to decide what to do, but in the end, Mum decided for me.

'Sorry, Megan,' she said. 'We only have one

spare seat belt. We can bring Alice, but I'm afraid we won't have room for your other friend.'

I didn't speak. It wasn't the time or the place to mention that Hazel was no friend of mine, and that if I never saw her again it would be too soon.

We all looked at Alice and waited to see what she had to say. Like me, she seemed to be having trouble making up her mind. At last she spoke.

'Thanks, Sheila, but I think I'll stay here – otherwise Hazel will be on her own for the day, and she'll be bored.'

'Her parents might show up,' I said.

Hazel made a face at me.

'They probably won't. Thanks for staying with me Alice.'

Then, before anyone could say anything else, she put her arm around Alice's shoulder and practically dragged her back into the school. I waved good-bye, but neither of them saw me.

Mum shook her head.

'What a pushy girl!' she said.

You don't know half of it, I thought as I climbed into the back of the car with Rosie. I wished I could tell Mum what was going on, but I knew it would have been a mistake. Mum would have dived in to try to sort everything out, and then everything would end up even worse than before. So I didn't say any more, as Dad revved up the car and we set off for our day out.

*   *   *

We had a lovely time. It was really warm so we decided to go to the beach. For a while I made sandcastles with Rosie, Dad read the paper, and Mum did her knitting. She was knitting something in thick, hard wool the colour of green slime. It was probably a surprise jumper for someone – a very scary surprise. I hoped it wasn't for me.

After a while, we were all hot and sweaty, so we decided to go for a swim. It was fun, once I got over the shock of seeing my family's swimming clothes. (After two weeks with normal people, I'd almost forgotten how weird my family was.) Mum's swimming togs were huge and covered with fading flowers. They looked like they had once belonged to her granny's granny. Poor Rosie was wearing a floppy bikini that looked suspiciously as if Mum had knitted it. (Luckily Rosie is too young to be as embarrassed as she should be by that sort of thing.) Dad was in horrible, tight shiny swimming trunks that made a lot of people stare at him, and two little boys laugh out loud.

We swam until we were all shivery and my fingers were turning white. Then we raced back to our stuff and wrapped ourselves in our towels and tried not to think cold thoughts.

When we were all dry and warm again, Mum started to root around in one of the huge bags she always seems to carry around with her.

'I've brought a picnic,' she said with a big grin – like that was something that would make us all jump up and down with joy.

First she pulled out a bag of bananas, but it looked like someone had sat on them. They were so badly squashed that even Mum (who thinks wasting food is almost as bad as killing someone) didn't try to insist that we eat them.

Next she rooted in another bag and produced a pack of (and I'm not joking here) chick-pea sandwiches. For the millionth time I wondered why I couldn't have had a mum who put normal stuff in sandwiches like ham or chicken or cheese. The sandwiches had been left lying in the sun, though, and they smelled so bad that even Dad wouldn't eat them. (And he'd eat practically anything).

'Oh well,' said Mum. 'Looks like we'll have to go straight on to our treat.' As she spoke she pulled out another package. 'It's my special sugar-free, fat-free cookies.'

I sighed. I should have known she wouldn't have brought a real treat. Mum's sugar-free, fat-free cookies were also taste-free – unless you think dried-up sawdust has a taste.

Rosie squealed.

'Yippee. Cookies,' she said, jumping in the air. As she landed, she knocked the package from Mum's hand and the cookies flew into the sand. For a minute I thought Rosie had done it deliberately, then I remembered that Rosie is so innocent, she actually likes Mum's cookies. The poor child doesn't know what real cookies are supposed to taste like.

'Ooops. Sorry, Mum,' she said.

So that was the end of Mum's picnic.

I tried not to look too happy.

'There's nothing for it,' said Mum. 'I'll have to walk to the nearest shop and buy us some food.'

I gulped. There was no telling what she'd bring back. There was every chance we'd end up sitting on the beach eating cold butter beans, or something totally gross like that.

Dad must have seen the scared look on my

face.

'No, Sheila,' he said. 'That wouldn't be fair. You were up early packing all that lovely food for us. You rest here with the girls, and I'll go and buy us something to eat.'

After Mum had spent twenty minutes telling him about the food pyramid, and hydrogenated fats and all that boring stuff, Dad set off for the shop.

Fifteen minutes later, he was back with a huge foil bag under his arm. As he came close, a beautiful smell wafted towards me. My mouth started to water – that definitely wasn't the smell of butter beans.

'Look what I got,' said Dad proudly, opening the bag so we could all see.

Mum actually went pale when she saw that the bag was full of potato wedges, chicken nuggets, and sausages.

'Sorry, love. It's all they had,' said Dad, but he winked at me when Mum wasn't looking, so I had a funny feeling he wasn't telling the complete truth.

Dad sat down and divided out the food. Mum kept going on about how bad it was for us, and how ashamed she'd be if any of her friends came along and saw her poisoning her family in public. I thought that it would serve her right if her family embarrassed her in public – at least she'd see how I spend most of my life. I didn't say that though – I was too busy picking non-organic meat off non-organic chicken bones.

Rosie ate loads of the wedges. I don't think she'd ever had anything like that before. She kept on patting her tummy, and saying 'yum-yum'.

Dad and I laughed, but Mum looked as if she'd love to grab what was left of the food and dump it in the nearest bin. She is so totally uptight when it comes to food.

In the end Dad said,

'Lighten up, Sheila. One bad meal won't kill the child.' And to our surprise, Mum did lighten up, and she even laughed at herself. And when she thought no-one was looking she ate three potato wedges and four chicken nuggets.

Chapter fourteen

It was nearly tea-time when I got back to camp. I hugged Rosie, then I got out of the car and closed the door behind me. Mum and Dad wound down their windows. Mum was building up for a big emotional farewell scene, but Dad was in a hurry home because there was a rugby match on the television later that he wanted to watch, so I was saved.

I stood in the driveway and waved as they drove off. Dad can be a bit of a pain sometimes, and Mum is a total embarrassment most of the time, but in a way it was nice and simple being around them. I could be myself, and I knew they loved me no matter what, and even if I said something stupid, they wouldn't go on and on about it forever. Sometimes it was easier than being with friends.

As soon as the car was gone from view, I went up to my room. There was no sign of Alice or Hazel. I walked around all the places I thought they could have been, but I couldn't find them anywhere. In the end, I found Gloria lying on a rug behind a hedge in the garden. She was rubbing sun protection cream into her arms. I was puzzled. Her skin was so dark already, it was hard to imagine the sun doing anything at all to it except making it nice and warm. She looked up and saw me. I didn't know if it was rude, but I had to ask.

'Are you hoping to get a tan?'

Gloria gave one of her big laughs.

'Do you think I look a bit pale?'

I could feel my face going red.

'No. I mean yes. I mean…'

Gloria laughed again.

'Black skin burns too you know,' she said.

I didn't know that. I felt a bit stupid so I said quickly,

'Have you seen Alice anywhere?'

Gloria nodded.

'Yes, I saw her just after you left this morning. Hazel's parents came to take her out, and they took Alice with them. They should be back soon.'

She stopped and then she said suddenly.

'Actually, I've just remembered they won't be back soon. Hazel's parents asked Mrs Duggan if they could keep the girls out for dinner.'

Great. Alice got to spend the whole day with Hazel and now they were hanging out in some fancy restaurant, while I was stuck at camp on my own.

Gloria sat up.

'Is everything OK Megan?' she asked.

I nodded, even though I felt like screaming or stamping my foot or crying or something.

Gloria patted the rug beside her and I felt I had to sit down.

'You and Alice are good friends, aren't you?'

I nodded again.

'It's tough when your friend makes other friends, isn't it?'

I nodded.

'Want my advice?'

I didn't know if I did want her advice. Gloria was very kind, and I knew she was trying to help, but I could still remember how she had tried to help me by telling Alice she had to be my partner in the talent show. That hadn't turned out very well, had it? But it would have been rude to say no, so I nodded yet again.

'Yes, please. Tell me what you think I should do.'

Gloria smiled at me. 'Just try to relax. If you and Alice are real good friends, it will take more than a few weeks at summer camp to ruin it.

Have fun with Alice, but don't crowd her. Hang out with the other kids too.'

But I *was* hanging out with the other kids. I liked Sarah, and Sam was good fun, but that wasn't enough.

All I really wanted was for Alice to still be my friend.

Only problem was – all Hazel wanted was for Alice not to be my friend.

'It'll all work out in end, you'll see.' Gloria lay back on her rug, and closed her eyes. I could tell that the conversation was over.

'Thanks Gloria,' I said in the happiest voice I could manage, and I went up to my room and waited for tea-time.

It was nearly nine o'clock by the time Alice and Hazel got back. I was up in my room, trying to read, but not able to concentrate. I heard them before I saw them – chatting and giggling like they'd known each other for ever, not for just a few weeks.

They burst into the room, all happy and excited. Alice was so wound-up she couldn't stop talking.

'Oh, Megan. We've had such a fun day,' she said. 'Hazel's family is sooo cool.'

Great. Trust Hazel to have a cool family, when I was stuck with the least cool family on the planet.

'They're just back from Dubai, you know,' continued Alice. 'And Hazel's brother is sooo funny. He's called Lee. He's Hazel's twin, but they don't look alike. He's *much* better looking than she is.'

Hazel gave her a kick in the leg, when she said this, but I was sorry to see that it was a friendly kind of kick. The kind of kick you only give to people you like.

Alice stopped to catch her breath, and then went on.

'Lee's friend came out with us too. He's called Conor. He's nice, but not as nice as Lee.' She gave a sly look towards Hazel.

'Hazel likes Conor, though. A lot.'

'But what about Jordan?' I blurted out at Hazel. 'I thought you liked Jordan.'

Hazel gave a bored sigh.

'Oh, Jordan,' she said. 'Jordan is so last week.'

Poor Jordan, I thought at first – before I realised that he was lucky Jordan to have escaped from the evil Hazel.

Alice gave a small laugh, and continued the account of her day.

'First we went bowling, and then we had lunch in this really cool place, and then we went out on a really cool boat because Hazel's dad knows the guy who owns it, and then we went to a really cool restaurant for dinner, and Lee and Conor played this real cool trick on the waiter, but he didn't mind, well not very much anyway, and ...'

And on and on and on she went. In the end I thought if she said the word 'cool' one more time, I'd have to jump up and punch her in the face or something. And all the time Hazel was watching her with a small smile on her face, like having such a 'cool' family was no big deal. (But she must have known it was. After all, she'd seen my family, and even a blind person couldn't call them cool.)

After ages, Alice must have noticed that I wasn't quite as enthusiastic about her day as she was. She stopped suddenly.

'Sorry, Megan,' she said. 'I've been going on a bit, haven't I?'

I was so happy that she'd stopped at last that I decided not to give her a hard time. 'It's OK,' I said. 'I'm glad you had a nice day.'

That was the truth actually. I *was* glad that she'd had a nice day. I just wasn't very glad that Hazel had been a part of it. I wished Alice could have had a nice day with me.

'Anyway,' Alice said. 'What about you? What did you do? Did you have a nice time with your family?'

What could I say to that?

I'd had a lovely day out. I'd had fun making endless sandcastles with Rosie, and swimming in the sea. Dad buying the chicken nuggets and the sausages and the potato wedges had been really funny. Still, I knew if I described my day to Alice and Hazel, it would suddenly sound stupid. My day would have sounded totally dull if you compared it with the fun day Alice and Hazel had.

I shrugged.

'It was OK I suppose. Parent stuff, you know, kind of boring.'

And Alice didn't ask me any more about it.

* * *

In bed that night, I kept hearing beeps and seeing flashes from Alice and Hazel's phones. At first I thought they were texting each other – telling each other secret stuff about their day out that they didn't want me to hear.

Then I had a horrible thought.

Were they writing stuff about me?

Was Hazel mocking me and my family?

And was Alice letting her?

For a while I pretended not to care. I listened to my Walkman. (I decided to take a chance, because it was dark, so Hazel couldn't see it.)

In the end though, I couldn't take it any more. I pretended I needed to go to the toilet, and when I got back into the bedroom, I kind of casually went and sat on Alice's bed. She was smiling to herself as she read her latest message.

'Who are you texting?' I asked, trying to sound like I didn't really care all that much – like it wasn't driving me totally crazy, wondering what was going on.

Alice looked up, as if she'd just remembered that I existed.

'Oh, hi Megan,' she said. 'It's just Conor and Lee. They are *soooo* funny. Look at this.'

She held the phone towards me and I read the message. It was very long, and was about a bowl of carrot soup and a slice of bread and it didn't make any sense at all to me.

Then Alice said,

'Oh, sorry, Meg. You wouldn't get that one. It's a joke about something Lee said today.'

She leaned out of bed, and held the phone over to Hazel. As soon as Hazel read the message she fell into a fit of laughing like it was the funniest thing she'd ever in her life read. I felt like throwing my uncool, ancient Walkman at her, because I knew that half the reason she was laughing was because she knew that I didn't get the joke.

I went back to my bed and climbed in. I heard my Walkman clatter down onto the floor. It sounded as if it might be broken.

I didn't care.

I didn't care about anything except that I had never in my whole life felt as left out of things as I did at that moment.

Chapter fifteen

Next morning I was kind of glad when the time came for Alice and Hazel to go off to their tennis course. I thought I'd scream if I had to hear another word about Conor or Lee or the 'cool' time they'd all had together.

After basketball, Sarah didn't feel well.

'I'm going to skip lunch,' she said. 'I think I'll go and lie down in bed for a while.'

'You poor thing,' I said, putting my arm around her. 'I hope it isn't anything too serious.'

She shook her head.

'I don't think so. I'm sure I'll be fine soon. Anyway, if it turns out to be anything bad, I'll make sure to breathe on Hazel so she catches it too.'

I laughed, and waved good-bye to her, and then set off for lunch.

I collected my food, and went to sit next to Alice and Hazel. I tried not to care that Alice kept talking to Hazel, and sometimes seemed to forget that I was even there.

By the time we were all finished our jelly and ice-cream though, I was more worried than ever. Not alone had Alice got totally caught up in her new friend's life, but also she had that funny gleam in her eye that always makes me feel so nervous. She was plotting and scheming again – I was sure of it.

The three of us sat outside in the sun for a while before we had to go to French. Alice and Hazel spent most of that time with their phones in their hands, texting madly, like it was going to go out of fashion any second. Then, during French, they kept giggling and grinning at each other. They were definitely up to something – I just wished they'd tell me what it was.

That night should have been fun. Gloria and the other leaders had set up a treasure hunt all around the school, and the winners were to get a big box of sweets to share. We were all ready to go when Gloria said the dreaded words,

'Now everyone, find a partner to hunt with.'

I wondered if she'd told Alice and Hazel that they couldn't go together, like she had for the talent show. I soon found out that she hadn't.

Before I could even move, Hazel grabbed Alice's arm, and said,

'Partners?'

Alice looked at me with a funny expression on her face.

Was she upset because she couldn't go with me?

Or did she just feel guilty because this time she'd got the partner she really wanted?

Luckily Sarah was feeling better, and she was standing near me. She came over.

'Will we go together?' she asked.

I nodded.

'Thanks,' I said, and tried not to watch as Hazel dragged Alice across the room and far away from me.

Two boys won the treasure hunt, but someone had seen them cheating, so it didn't really count. Anyway, there were enough sweets for everyone, and there was silence for at least ten minutes while we all chewed happily.

Sarah and I hung out together for a while when the treasure hunt was over. I couldn't really concentrate on what she was saying though, because I was too busy trying to see where Alice and Hazel had got to. Sarah was being really nice, and I didn't want to offend her, so I said I was going to go and have an early night.

I found Alice and Hazel up in our bedroom. They were huddled together on Alice's bed, whispering and laughing.

When I walked in, Hazel jumped up, looking

really guilty. Alice just laughed.

'It's OK,' she said. 'You don't have to worry about Megan. We can trust her.'

I was glad she felt that way, and that she wanted to include me. But what exactly did I need to be trusted with?

Alice grabbed my arms and pulled me until I was sitting on the bed. Hazel sat down on the other side of me.

'We have a plan,' said Alice, and that old familiar sinking feeling hit me right in the middle of my tummy. Alice's plans always ended up being more trouble than they were worth.

'There's a really funny film out at the moment,' she continued. 'And tomorrow afternoon we're going to go to and see it.'

That didn't sound so bad. How serious could a trip to the cinema be? My tummy began to unsink itself.

'That's great,' I said. 'I haven't been to the cinema in ages. Has Gloria arranged it?'

Hazel gave a mean laugh.

'No, Dork-face. Your precious Gloria hasn't arranged it. She doesn't know anything about it. We're sneaking out of camp.'

My mouth fell open. I knew I probably looked really stupid, but I couldn't help it.

'Sneaking out?'

My voice was all squeaky and scared. Even thinking about sneaking out made me afraid.

Would I ever be brave enough to actually do it?

Hazel gave another mean laugh.

'Yeah, sneaking out. See Alice? I knew you shouldn't tell little scaredy-cat Megan.'

Alice stood up.

'That's not fair, Hazel. Don't say that. We can trust Megan, can't we, Meg?'

I nodded weakly.

I took a deep breath, and put on my bravest voice.

'Tell me everything. I want to know every single detail.'

Before Alice could say anything, there was a tap on the door, and Gloria peeped in.

'Girls, you should all be in bed by now,' she said in a pretend cross voice. 'Lights out in four minutes.'

There was a big scramble as we got ready for bed, and then Gloria's hand appeared around the door, and switched out the light.

I waited a few minutes to be sure that Gloria was gone. Then I whispered.

'OK, Al. Tell me what the big plan is.'

'OK,' began Alice, but just then her phone beeped, and for the next ten minutes she and Hazel texted madly, giggling to each other as they did so. By the time Alice finally put down her phone, I was almost asleep. I jerked myself awake though.

'OK, Al,' I said. 'Now tell me about the big plan.'

She gave a big yawn.

'Sorry, Meg,' she said. 'How about I tell you

tomorrow? I'm really tired right now.'

'I suppose so,' I said, trying not to sound too disappointed.

I felt like punching someone. I *hated* that Hazel knew all the details of the plan and I didn't. I was supposed to be Alice's best friend. I was the one she was supposed to share her secret plans with first.

I couldn't argue though. I didn't want Hazel to see Alice and me fighting. Still it wouldn't have mattered anyway. Alice is the world champion secret-keeper. I'd have to wait until the next day, whether I liked it or not.

Even though I was tired, I hardly slept at all that night. All kinds of thoughts and questions raced around my brain.

I wanted to know more, yet at the same time, I didn't want to.

How would we sneak out?

What would happen if we were caught?

Did I want to see any film so much that I'd risk

being sent to Mrs Duggan, or worse, being sent home from camp in disgrace?

I could just say I didn't want to go with Alice and Hazel.

But then I thought – I had to go with them. This was my big chance to prove myself. It would let Alice know that I wasn't just a quiet little chicken. And it would let Hazel know that I wasn't just going to stand back and let her ruin my friendship with Alice.

A few sleepless hours later, I had made up my mind.

For once in my life I was going to be brave.

I was going to break all the rules, and have some fun.

I felt a bit better once I'd decided.

Sneaking out would be fun.

Maybe Alice would lend me the turquoise top she'd promised me for the disco.

I wondered if I'd have time to straighten my hair.

Would Hazel do my face again?

Luckily my best jeans were clean.

Maybe …

When I finally fell asleep I had lots of crazy mixed up dreams about Alice, Hazel and me..

Chapter sixteen

We all slept late in the morning, so there was no chance to talk about the plan. At breakfast time, Sarah came and sat with us, so we couldn't say anything then either. I'd have liked to tell Sarah that we were going to sneak out. Maybe she'd even want to come with us. But I knew Hazel wouldn't want that, and I didn't want to risk making her mad. So I didn't say anything.

After breakfast, Alice and Hazel had to off to their tennis lessons. Just before they left, Alice came and whispered in my ear. 'I'll tell you every-thing later, OK?'

I nodded.

Basketball seemed to go on forever. I was so excited and scared. A few times I missed really easy shots, and the coach got cross with me.

'Want me to spit in his coffee later?' whispered Sam. It was funny, but I was too nervous to laugh properly.

In the morning break, Sarah and I sat together, but I couldn't concentrate on what she was saying – I was too busy telling myself to be brave for the afternoon's adventures.

At last it was lunch break. While everyone else was tidying up the basketballs and the team vests, I raced upstairs to my room. Alice and Hazel weren't there yet. I changed into my jeans, and borrowed Alice's hair-straightener and straightened my hair. I took her top out from the wardrobe, and put it on. I knew she wouldn't mind. Then I sat on my bed and waited.

At last Alice and Hazel came clattering up the stairs. They came into the room and closed the door behind them. Alice looked at me.

'Hey, Megan, that top really suits you,' she said. 'You look great, but why…..?'

Hazel didn't let her finish her question. 'Come on, Alice. Hurry up and get ready. We have to go in ten minutes, otherwise we'll miss our bus.'

I grinned at her.

'You don't have to worry about me,' I said. 'I'm ready.'

Alice gave me a funny look.

'Ready for what?' she asked.

I laughed.

'For the big sneaking-out adventure, of course.'

Alice was still looking at me in that strange way, but she didn't say anything.

'Come on, Al,' I said. 'Don't keep me in suspense any more. Tell me how we're going to get away with this.'

Alice didn't answer. It took me a minute to notice that Hazel was sniggering at me, and that Alice had a look on her face like I had punched her really hard right between the eyes.

There was a silence. A very, very, very long silence. I twiddled my straight hair, and rubbed imaginary dust from the leg of my jeans.

Finally Hazel broke the silence with a big loud laugh.

'Ha,' she said. 'Surely you don't think that you're coming?'

I could feel my face going bright red. Of course I was going with them. That had always been the plan, hadn't it?

I looked at Alice desperately.

Surely she wouldn't let me down.

Would she?

Alice's face was red too. She looked kind of mixed-up, but still she didn't say anything. Usually she didn't know how to stop talking, so why was she suddenly so quiet?

'Tell her,' Hazel sneered. 'Tell your little friend everything. Or do you want me to?'

Alice's face was so red I thought that maybe you could make toast by holding bread up to it. I had never seen her look so embarrassed before.

She didn't look at me.

'You see, Meg ...' she began.

This was all wrong. I could feel that hot feeling behind my eyes that meant tears weren't far behind.

Hazel gave a huge snort of laughter.

'Megan really thought she was coming with us. I don't believe it. That is so totally pathetic.'

I quickly wiped away the first tear with the back of my hand. Unfortunately, Hazel saw it.

'Oh, stop crying and get over yourself, Megan,' she said.

I wiped away another tear and looked desperately at Alice.

'Let me come with you,' I begged.

Alice shook her head.

'I'm sorry, Meg,' she said. 'This is really awkward. You see … I mean … it's …'

Then the words came rushing out.

'What I mean is …… you can't come with us. I'd like you to, but you can't.'

I still didn't understand.

'But why can't I come?' I asked. 'You know I won't tell anyone.'

Alice hesitated.

'Well, you see, it's a … it's kind of a date.'

Now it was my turn to be embarrassed.

'A date?' I repeated.

Hazel laughed an evil laugh.

'Yes, a date. You know, like with you and Sam.'

She stopped and put her hand over her mouth.

'Oh, silly me, I forgot. You and Sam didn't go on a date, did you? Anyway, a date is where a boy and a girl go out together. Only in this case it's two boys and two girls. Conor and Lee and Alice and me. Four is a lovely even number, don't you think? So I'm afraid there's no place for you. You stay here with your sweet little summer-camp friend, Sarah, while Al and I go have fun in the real world.'

I couldn't believe what I was hearing.

Alice was going on a date, and I was only hearing about it now?

How had this happened?

By now Hazel was ready. I had to admit that she looked really great in a short denim skirt and a striped top. She was looking at her watch and tapping her foot impatiently.

Alice was tying the laces of her new runners.

She looked up at Hazel.

'Why don't you wait for me outside the back door? I'll be down in a few minutes.'

Hazel shrugged.

'Whatever?' she said, and she went out of the room. 'Just don't be late for our important date.'

Alice came and sat on my bed. She put her arm around me.

'I'm so sorry, Megan,' she said. 'I thought you

knew that it was just Hazel and me. I had no idea that you thought you were coming too.'

I didn't answer for a minute. I was all mixed-up.

Part of me was disappointed that I wasn't getting to go on the big adventure.

Part of me was very relieved that I wasn't going on the big adventure.

Mostly though, I just felt stupid for having thought that I was invited in the first place.

I should have known that I was never going to be included in any plan that involved Hazel.

'Meg, I'm really so sorry,' said Alice again.

I knew that she meant it. Suddenly I understood that this wasn't really Alice's fault. She was my best friend, and she was all excited about her big date, and I should be happy for her.

I tried to smile.

'So I'm not going with you. It's not a big deal really. Tell me all about it anyway,' I said. 'Tell me what you and Hazel plan to do.'

She smiled at me.

'After all the crazy stuff you and I did this year, this should be very easy. We just climb over the back wall while everyone else is still at lunch. Then we walk into the village. There's a bus into Cork at one o'clock – Hazel phoned up and checked. We're meeting Lee and Conor outside the cinema – Hazel was there before and knows the way. The four of us go and watch the film, then we hang out for a while, and get something to eat, and then we get the bus back. Like I said – it's easy-peasy.'

'But won't someone miss you?'

She shook her head.

'No. We've got it all worked out. Gloria was on lunch and tea duty yesterday, so she won't be on again today. They only do every second day. And the other leaders won't miss us. They don't even know us properly. And after lunch it's rehearsals for the French play, and Hazel and I aren't in it, so we won't be missed then either. And we'll be back long before Gloria comes to check up on us at bed-time. And that's it – that's the plan.'

She was right. It did sound easy. I tried not to think about how all of Alice's plans sounded easy until the time came to carry them out. In the end, they were always much more complicated than I could ever have imagined.

'But why?' I asked.

Alice gave a dreamy kind of smile.

'It's because of Lee. He's really nice. And I want to see him again. And if I don't do this, I won't get another chance. He's going to America with his family next Sunday and we'll be going back home to Limerick. It's now or never.'

She looked at her watch and jumped up.

'I've got to go or we'll miss the bus. Thanks for understanding.'

Did I understand?

I'm not really sure.

I fiddled with the embroidered sleeve of the top I was wearing. Alice smiled.

'That top really does suit you,' she said. 'You can wear it whenever you like. You can wear it again for the disco. We'll have a great night then, I promise.'

I smiled back at her, and then she skipped out of the room. I could hear her singing as she went down the stairs.

I was glad someone was happy.

I took off Alice's top, and threw it into the back of the wardrobe. Then I changed into my own faded and stretched old t-shirt, and went downstairs for my lunch.

Chapter seventeen

It seemed like a very long afternoon. I kept on thinking of Alice – where she was, and what she was doing, and was she having such a good time with Hazel that she'd never want to be friends with me again?

After lunch Sarah and I watched the rehearsals for the French play, and then we played rounders with some of the others. After that we just hung out.

I really, really wanted to tell Sarah about Alice

and Hazel sneaking out. But even though I knew I could trust Sarah, something stopped me. I was afraid that somehow Hazel would find out, and then she would make my life even more of a misery for the last few days of the camp.

At tea-time, as Alice had predicted, there was no sign of Gloria, and the other group leaders didn't notice that they were missing two girls. Sarah noticed immediately though.

'Where's Alice? And Hazel?' she asked as we sat down with our trays. 'I haven't seen them all afternoon.'

I had an answer ready for this.

'Oh, Hazel didn't feel very well, so she's up in the bedroom. Alice stayed with her. They might be down later.'

Sarah shrugged.

'Somehow I can't make myself feel sorry for Hazel. Let's hope whatever is wrong with her will keep her out of our way for the next few days.'

I giggled.

'Well, if she gets better too soon, we can send Sam to spit in her drink, and she might have a relapse.'

When tea was over, we went in to the television room, and watched two DVDs in a row. As usual, there were rows between the boys and the girls about what we should watch. In the end each group picked one DVD, and we had fun mocking the others' choices.

By the time the DVDs were over, it was almost time for bed. I told Sarah that I was tired, and went up to my room.

I lay on my bed and tried to read my book. I couldn't concentrate though. I kept thinking about Alice and Hazel. I was starting to get a bit nervous. It was getting late. I was sure they should be back by now. What if Gloria came to say good-night and Alice and Hazel weren't here?

What would Gloria say?

What would I say?

How would I cover for them?

After a while, I could hear all the other girls coming upstairs and getting ready for bed. Soon Gloria would be around. Usually I liked it when Gloria came to say good-night. Tonight though, I was dreading it.

I was starting to feel a bit sick. Alice and Hazel would be in soooo much trouble if they didn't get back soon.

I turned back to my book and stared at the same page for ages, without reading a single word. Then I threw the book onto the ground. This whole thing was just too awful. I wished I was with Alice and Hazel instead of stuck here worrying about them.

A little bit later I heard Gloria's big loud laugh. She was at the other end of the corridor, checking that everyone was tucked up in bed. My heart started to beat really fast.

I had to do something.

But what could I do?

Alice would have known what to do, but that wasn't much use to me, was it?

Think, I whispered to myself. *Think. Think.*

I slapped myself on the forehead, hoping that if there were any stray ideas lurking inside my head, it might make them pop out.

Suddenly inspiration struck. I jumped off my bed, raced to the wardrobe, and grabbed big heaps of clothes. I pulled back Alice's bedclothes and tried to make a person-shape out of a bundle of clothes. Then I did the same to Hazel's bed. It didn't look very convincing (well actually it didn't look at all convincing), but it was the best I could do in about fifteen seconds. I just had to hope that Gloria wouldn't look too closely. Then I switched out the light and jumped into my own bed with my clothes on.

A second later the bedroom door opened. I shut my eyes and pretended to be asleep – I so didn't want to have to answer any awkward questions. I held my breath and hoped that Gloria wouldn't hear my heart thumping.

There was a moment's silence, and then I heard Gloria laugh softly.

'Girls these days. No stamina.' I coughed so that she'd know that at least there was someone alive in the room, but it didn't matter anyway. Gloria was gone. I'd saved Alice and Hazel. For a while at least.

I lay in bed for a long time. Now it was getting really late and I was getting really worried.

Where were they?

Why hadn't they come back?

Had something awful happened to them?

I always laugh at my mum, telling her that she always thinks the worst. Now I knew how she felt though. I was sure that something dreadful had happened to Alice and Hazel, and in a crazy way, I felt guilty, like somehow it was going to be my fault.

After a while, I got out of bed and looked at

Alice's alarm clock. It was nearly ten o'clock. I tip-toed out of my room, and down the corridor to Sarah's room. She was in bed, but still awake. Luckily the two other girls in her room were snoring softly. I whispered to Sarah,

'I need a loan of your phone.'

She sat up.

'Megan? What's going on? It's the middle of the night. What do you want a phone for?'

This wasn't the time for explanations, so I gave her the excuse I'd prepared.

'I'm homesick.' I whispered. 'I want to phone my mum.'

'You poor thing,' said Sarah. 'Of course you can borrow my phone. It's on the chair over there. You can bring it back in the morning. Don't talk too long – my credit's nearly gone.'

'Thanks, Sarah,' I whispered.

I took the phone and tip-toed back to my room.

Why hadn't I thought of that earlier?

In a few seconds I'd be talking to Alice. She'd tell me where she was, and why she was delayed, and everything would be OK.

I sat on my bed and dialled Alice's number. Even the ringing tone made me feel better. Then I got the dreaded message – *Hi, It's Alice. You've missed me, but try again later.*

I sighed. What was the point of having a phone if you hardly ever turned it on?

Hazel had a phone too of course, but I had no idea of her number, and no idea how to find it out.

I put the phone down.

Now what?

I sat on my bed and worried some more.

Alice and Hazel could be hurt.

Something awful might have happened to them.

And if I didn't tell someone, no-one would know, and no-one would go to help them.

But if I told on them, and then it turned out

that they were OK, neither of them would ever forgive me. Hazel didn't like me anyway, so that didn't matter so much. But Alice? What would I do if Alice hated me?

I looked at Alice's clock again. Fifteen minutes, I decided. If they weren't back in fifteen minutes, I'd have to go and tell someone..

Chapter eighteen

T hose fifteen minutes went veeeeery sloooooowly. Every time there was a creak on the stairs, or a footstep in the corridor or the sound of a door closing, I sat up in bed, hoping that it was Alice and Hazel coming back. But it never was.

At last the fifteen minutes were up.

I stood up and went to the door.

Then I went back and sat down again. Ten minutes, I decided. I could wait ten more minutes.

So I waited ten more long minutes, and still there was no sign of Alice and Hazel. I couldn't delay any more. I knew it was time to do something.

I went out into the corridor. It was deserted, and a bit creepy. I tip-toed as far as Sarah's room. This would be so much easier if she was there to support me. I raised my hand to tap on her door and then stopped myself. It wasn't fair to involve her in all of this. It was my mess, not hers. So I continued my lonely journey along the corridor.

I knew that the group leaders' rooms were all on the first floor. I tip-toed down the stairs, and along the corridor. I quickly found the door with Gloria's name on it. Under her name was a smiley face, and the words, 'knock if you need me.' I needed her, but still I was afraid. This was all much too hard.

I stood outside Gloria's door for a moment. I could hear music coming from her room. Lively, happy music. Just the opposite of the way I felt.

What would she say?

What would she do?

Was I about to make the biggest mistake of my whole life?

I took a deep breath, then I knocked on the door. There was no answer. I waited a minute, and then I knocked again, louder this time. Still no answer. I knocked a third time, louder than ever. Just as I did so, the song came to an end and my knock sounded really loud, almost loud enough to wake up the entire school.

Gloria came to the door with a book in her hand and her usual big smile on her face. She looked surprised to see me.

'Megan? What is it? Are you sick?'

I shook my head. Now that I was standing outside Gloria's bedroom, I didn't know exactly what to say. Gloria shook me gently by the shoulder.

'Talk to me, Megan. Something tells me this isn't just a friendly visit. What's wrong?'

At first I couldn't talk, but seconds later I couldn't stop. Everything came out in a rush.

'It's Alice. And Hazel,' I said. 'They sneaked out of camp. And they haven't come back. But they've been gone for ages. And I didn't know what to do. I'm so afraid that something dreadful has happened to them. What if they've been kidnapped? What if they're dead? And if they're not dead, I will be, because they'll kill me when they discover that I told you. They went to the pictures. In Cork. But they should be back by now. They should have been back ages ago. I'm so afraid, Gloria.'

The smile had faded from Gloria's face long before I had finished speaking.

'When did they go?' she asked.

'Just before lunch.'

Now Gloria's face was really serious. She threw her book into the bedroom, and stepped into the corridor, closing the door behind her.

'Now Megan, don't you worry. I'll deal with

this. I'll have to go and talk to Mrs Duggan.'

Mrs Duggan? I so did not want to get Mrs Duggan involved in this. Now I was sure I'd done the wrong thing. Alice would never, ever, ever forgive me.

It was as if Gloria could read my mind.

'Telling me was the right thing to do, Megan. Alice and Hazel are probably perfectly fine, but we need to be sure. We can't take any chances. Now you run along to bed, and stop worrying. I'll take care of everything.'

Gloria walked quickly towards the stairs, and out of sight. I stood for a few minutes, wishing I was at home, or at school, or even at the dentist – anywhere but there in that silent empty corridor.

Then I went back to my room, and got into bed.

What else could I do?

A few minutes later, I could hear whispering and giggling out in the corridor. Very familiar whispering and giggling.

My heart sank. All of a sudden I wasn't glad

that my friend was back. I was almost sad that something bad hadn't happened to her, because now I knew for sure that something bad was going to happen to me.

The door opened and Alice and Hazel tiptoed into the room. Alice reached for the light switch, but Hazel pulled her hand back.

'Don't put on the light,' she whispered. 'Do you want us to get into trouble?'

I gulped. They were already in very serious trouble, and it was all my fault.

I sat up in bed. Alice saw me and came and sat next to me.

'Meg, I'm glad you're still awake. Oh, we've had the best time ever. The film was *so* funny. You'd have loved it. I'll go and see it again with you when we get back to Limerick, if you like. And then we went for burgers. Lee and Conor know all these cool places in Cork. And then we just hung out in the park doing nothing really, but it was still fun. And we were enjoying ourselves so much, we forgot about the time, and we missed the last bus home, and we had to walk the whole way, and it's miles and miles. I've got a huge blister on my foot. If it doesn't get better quickly I so won't be able to dance at the disco. Did anyone notice that we were gone? Did Gloria say anything? What did you say to her? And Lee is soooo nice. You'd really like him. He said…'

And on and on she went, as only Alice can when she's excited about something. And I said nothing, because what could I say? And then, it didn't matter anyway because the door opened and the light went on and there were Gloria and Mrs Duggan and two other group leaders, and none of them looked very happy. And Alice looked at me in surprise, and Hazel leaned over to me, and gave me the most evil look I'd ever seen in my whole life and whispered,

'I'll get you for this.'

Then Mrs Duggan beckoned with her finger

and everyone except for me followed her out of
the room, and I sat on my bed and waited some
more.

Chapter nineteen

Much, much later the bedroom door opened again. Alice and Hazel came in with Gloria. The two girls didn't look cool and sophisticated any more. They had red blotchy faces, and Hazel had a big black streak of mascara down one cheek.

Gloria spoke sharply to them.

'Take your toothbrushes and towels and go down to the bathroom. Be back here in three minutes.'

The girls picked up their stuff and left the room without saying anything. Gloria came and sat on my bed. I started to cry. I couldn't help it. Gloria pulled a big flowery hanky from her pocket and handed it to me.

'It's clean. I promise,' she said.

I wiped away my tears, but it didn't make any difference. Lots more came to take their place. They dripped down my face and on to my bedcovers.

'What's going to happen to Alice and Hazel?' I asked.

Gloria sighed.

'They did a very silly thing, and they have to be punished. They're lucky they're not being sent home. Mrs Duggan is writing to their parents, of course. And instead of activities, Alice and Hazel are going to have detention after tea in the evening. Every evening.'

I gasped.

'But what about the disco?'

The disco was the highlight of the camp. Everyone had been looking forward to it since the day we'd arrived.

Gloria shook her head.

'I'm afraid they're going to miss the disco.'

'Alice is going to hate me forever,' I sobbed.

Gloria stroked my hair.

'She might for a little while. But she'll get over it.'

Just then Alice and Hazel came back into the room. Gloria stood up.

'Straight to bed, you two,' she said, in a voice very different to the one she'd used to me. 'And not a peep out of either of you.'

She looked at Alice.

'Don't you dare give Megan a tough time about this. She was worried about you. She was trying to be a good friend. And sometimes being a good friend means doing hard stuff.'

Alice didn't answer. Hazel gave me an evil look. Gloria went out of the room, and I could hear the slap-slap of her flip-flops as she went downstairs. I felt like running after her, and begging her to stay with me, to protect me. It wouldn't have helped though. Sooner or later I'd have to face up to what I had done.

Alice and Hazel began to change into their pyjamas. Neither of them looked at me.

'I'm sorry,' I said softly.

Still neither girl looked at me.

'I'm sorry,' I said again, a bit louder this time.

Still there was no response. I got out of bed and went over to Alice.

'I'm sorry, Al,' I said. 'I wasn't trying to get you into trouble. I was worried about you. That's all. I was afraid something bad had happened to you.'

Hazel interrupted.

'Something bad *did* happen to her. She met you.'

'Al, please listen,' I continued. 'Please, please listen to me. I didn't mean to get you into trouble. Honestly I didn't.'

Suddenly Alice turned to face me.

'But you *did* get me into trouble, didn't you? I am so dead when I get home. I'll probably be grounded for the rest of the summer. And the rest of the week is going to be no fun now. Everything is ruined, and it's all your fault.'

'But why?' I asked. 'Why do you think I'd deliberately get you into trouble?'

Alice pretended to think.

'Oh, I know,' she said. 'Maybe it's because you were jealous of me and Hazel having a good time. You wanted to get back at me and you found the perfect way.'

I started to cry again.

'That is so not what happened. I tried to help you.'

I pointed to the bundles of clothes under her bedclothes.

'Look, I even tricked Gloria when she came to say goodnight. I made it look like you were here. I wanted to help you, but in the end I was scared.

You're my friend and I was worried about you.'

Hazel stepped towards us.

'Ignore her, Alice. She thinks she can get back with you just by stuffing a bundle of clothes in your bed. She probably did that after she went telling tales to Gloria. I don't think you should talk to her.'

Alice tossed her head.

'Don't worry. I won't. Ever.'

I got into bed.

'You're not even trying to understand what happened. It's not fair,' I cried.

Hazel gave a cruel laugh.

'Life's not fair. Get over it.'

Chapter twenty

The next day was totally awful.

When we woke up, Alice and Hazel acted as if I wasn't in the room. They chatted about the fun they had had on their date, and all the cool stuff they'd done with Conor and Lee. Then they went on and on about how they didn't care about stupid camp activities, and that the camp disco was only for stupid babies anyway.

I tried talking to Alice a few times, but each time she just turned away.

I sat with Sarah for breakfast, as far away from Alice and Hazel as I could manage. Most of the kids had some idea that something had happened the evening before, but Alice, Hazel and I were the only ones who knew exactly what it had been.

When most of the other kids had gone to get ready for activities, Sarah asked me what was going on. I hesitated, but then decided that I had nothing left to lose, and told her the whole story. She listened without saying a word.

'You poor thing,' she said, when I had finished.

'What would you have done?' I asked.

Sarah didn't even hesitate.

'I'd have done exactly what you did.'

I'll never know if she was telling the truth, but it made me feel a bit better anyway.

'Come on,' said Sarah, giving me a quick hug. 'Try and forget about it for a while. Let's go and get ready for basketball.'

I hoped that by lunch-time, Alice might have calmed down a bit, and that I could get a chance to explain my side of the story to her. There was no real hope though – now Hazel acted as if she owned Alice. Everywhere one went, the other followed, almost as if they were attached to each other by an invisible string.

And so the day dragged on. I think Sarah told Sam what had happened, because he was especially nice to me. He was so nice that I even began to feel a bit better for a while. That only lasted till Alice and Hazel walked by though, pointing at me and laughing, and then I felt as bad as ever.

Sarah stayed with me the whole time – a bit like my own personal bodyguard. She was really funny, and kept trying to cheer me up. It wasn't the same as being with Alice, though. I'd only had one really bad fight with her before, when I was staying in Dublin, and she was trying to get rid of the man she thought was her mum's boyfriend. Even that had only lasted for a short while though. We said really mean things to each other, but after half an hour we were best friends again – probably better friends than ever before.

This time I didn't think it was going to turn out like that, though. As long as Hazel was around, she was going to do her very best to keep Alice and me apart. And by the time camp was over, Alice might have got so used to hating me, that she'd never, ever stop.

After tea, I went up to my room for a while. Alice and Hazel were downstairs in one of the classrooms, being watched over by a very cross Gloria. I sat on my bed and played with the tiny silver bus on a chain that Alice had given me during the spring break. We were very, very best friends then. And now it looked like that would never happen again.

The whole thing was so totally unfair – I'd only been trying to help Alice. The worst thing was, I'd often got into trouble because of Alice, but I always forgave her in the end. So why couldn't she forgive me?

For a while, I thought about phoning home. If

I told Mum and Dad how upset I was, maybe they'd let me come home. Home would have been much better than camp now that Alice and I were fighting. Even with all the porridge and organic vegetables, home suddenly seemed like a great place to be.

Then I got sense though. Mum would have been sympathetic, but she's a great believer in sticking things out, and after paying so much money for the camp, it would kill her if I left early. Dad might have been more understanding, but I knew he'd do whatever Mum said in the end.

So I was trapped.

I was public enemy number one, as far as Alice was concerned, and I couldn't do a single thing to change it.

Chapter twenty-one

And so the days went very, very slowly by. In the day-time, I stayed away from Alice and Hazel as much as possible. That wasn't too hard anyway as they were doing their very best to stay away from me. The camp wasn't all that big though, and despite our best efforts, we often bumped in to each other. Then they acted like I smelled bad, and skipped off, giggling and holding their noses.

The worst thing was, I still had to share a room with Alice and Hazel, so every night after nine o'clock it was just the three of us trapped inside the small room. I felt like a kitten being forced to share with two angry wolves.

As soon as lights went out every night, I got into bed, and cried myself to sleep. At first I tried to cry quietly, afraid that if Alice and Hazel heard me, they'd start mocking me. It didn't matter though. They just went on with their lives as if they could neither see nor hear me. In the bedroom at night, they were so busy texting Conor and Lee, and swapping iPods, that I could have stood in the middle of the floor and jumped up and down and shrieked at the top of my voice, and still they'd have acted as if I didn't exist.

On the third day after the sneaking out day, Gloria called me aside after lunch.

'You and I need to talk,' she said.

She led me into a quiet corner of the garden, and sat beside me on a bench. At first she talked about trivial kind of stuff, but I knew what she was building up to. It didn't take her very long.

'Is Alice giving you a hard time?' she asked.

How could I answer that?

Alice was giving me a hard time – a very, very hard time.

But was it fair to tell on her?

Gloria folded her arms.

'I'll take that as a yes, then,' she said.

I still didn't know what to say. Even though Alice was being totally mean, I didn't want to get her into even more trouble.

'Would you like me to have a word with her?' asked Gloria.

At last I was able to answer.

'No way. I mean no. No thanks.'

Gloria smiled at me.

'I can be very delicate. She wouldn't have to know that I've spoken to you.'

I shook my head.

'She'll figure it out. She's not stupid. And if

she thinks I told you she was being mean to me, she'll find a way to hate me even more than she does already.'

Gloria sighed.

'Poor Megan. Life doesn't always seem fair, does it?'

I shook my head.

'That's what Hazel said too.'

Gloria gave a small chuckle.

'Well, Megan, between you and me, I think it's less fair than usual when there are girls like Hazel around.'

I tried to smile. Gloria patted my hand.

'Maybe you should just give Alice more time.'

'But she's had three days. Camp will be over, and she'll still hate me.'

'Well, I know it doesn't seem like it now, but in the great scheme of things, this camp won't turn out to have been so important,' said Gloria. 'You and Alice will get home, and in a few days, it will be like none of this happened.'

I didn't answer. Clearly Gloria didn't know Alice as well as I did. Alice could be the most stubborn person in the world when it suited her.

Gloria stood up.

'You just stick with Sarah for a while. She's a nice girl. And Sam …' she hesitated and gave me a funny look before continuing. '… is it just me or are you and Sam especially friendly?'

I knew I was going red.

Gloria laughed.

'It's OK, you don't have to answer that one,' she said. 'And come talk with me, if things get too much for you. I'm always available.'

Gloria went back inside and I stayed sitting on the bench for a while. It was a beautiful day, and the sun was warm on my face. I even started to feel a bit better for a while, but then Alice and Hazel went past, arm in arm, and everything seemed just as bad as before.

Chapter twenty-two

Next day, (as if things weren't bad enough), was the day of the disco.

When I woke up, Alice and Hazel were already awake. They were lying on Alice's bed, texting as usual. As soon as Hazel saw that I was awake, she started her daily attack on me.

'Oh look. Baby's awake,' she said in a silly voice. 'Baby must be all excited about the baby disco.'

I turned my face to the wall, but Hazel went on anyway.

'I wonder has baby got a nice new dress for the

disco? And a pretty pink ribbon for her little baby hair?'

Alice didn't say anything which made me feel a small bit better, but she didn't ask Hazel to stop either. She just kept her eyes on her phone, texting as if her life depended on it.

I got dressed as quickly as I could, and ran down to breakfast. Everyone was all excited about the disco. Even the boys were talking about what they were going to wear.

I picked up my food, and brought my tray to where Sarah was sitting. I sat down next to her. She was all excited too.

'I am *so* looking forward to the disco,' she said. 'I'm going to wear my denim skirt, and a white shirt, and this really cool sparkly belt my mum gave me for my birthday.'

I sighed. Why couldn't I have the kind of mum who gave really cool sparkly belts as birthday presents? On my last birthday my mum had given me a book about gardening, four new pairs of socks, and a voucher for the local swimming pool.

Sarah interrupted my thoughts.

'What are you wearing tonight?'

I gave another big sigh. A week ago, I'd had it all planned. Now I had no idea. I had a funny feeling that Alice wouldn't want to lend me the turquoise top that she'd promised me. I still had my white jeans, but all my tops seemed old and raggy. Everyone would look great, and I'd be like Cinderella – before her fairy godmother arrived.

Anyway, it didn't matter, because I'd suddenly made up my mind.

'I'm not going to the disco tonight,' I said quickly.

Sarah looked at me in horror.

'But you have to go to the disco. Everyone's going.'

I shrugged.

'Alice and Hazel aren't going.'

'Yeah, but that's only because they're not

allowed to.'

I shrugged again, like I didn't really care. 'Whatever.'

We were quiet for a minute, and then Sarah said, 'Are they talking to you yet?'

I shook my head.

Sarah made a face.

'Why can't they just get over themselves?'

I had to smile.

'I don't care about Hazel,' I said. 'I don't care if she ever talks to me or not. But I wish Alice would be friends with me again.'

Sarah smiled at me.

'She will. Don't worry. When you get back home, and Alice is far away from Horrible Hazel, everything will be like before. Anyway, back to the disco. If you don't go, it's like showing Alice and Hazel that they've won. They'll know that they've really upset you. You have to go tonight, just to show them that you don't care.'

'But I do care,' I protested.

Sarah smiled again.

'Well then you just have to pretend that you don't. Now finish your breakfast, and come up to my room. I've got lots of clothes, and I'll lend you something for tonight.'

On the way up to Sarah's room, we met Hazel. To my horror, she was wearing Alice's turquoise top. I knew already that I wouldn't be wearing it any time soon, but it really hurt to see it on Hazel – especially since it looked so good on her.

'Like my top?' she said. 'My best friend Alice lent it to me.'

Sarah laughed.

'It's a lovely top, and you're very lucky to have it. Are you wearing it to detention tonight?'

Hazel tossed her head, and flounced off.

I smiled.

Why could I never think of quick replies like that?

Why did my clever comments only ever come to me when it was hours too late?

*　　*　　*

Sarah is probably the kindest person I've ever met. She lent me a beautiful red t-shirt, and a really cool pair of jeans, and a pair of red sandals. She did my hair for me, and lent me some sparkly lip-gloss.

We met Sam on the way in to the disco, and he said,

'You look really nice, Megan,' Luckily it was a bit dark, so no-one could see how red I went.

All through the disco Sarah stayed with me (except for the three times that Sam asked me to dance) and she included me with all of her school-friends, and bought me two drinks and some crisps. And she never even let on that she was bored when I kept saying how nice Sam was.

And yet all the time, I kept wishing that it was Alice who was standing beside me, that it was Alice telling me jokes, that it was Alice and me having the fun night that we'd been dreaming of ever since we'd signed up for summer camp weeks and weeks earlier.

When the disco was over, we were allowed to stay up for another half an hour. Sarah and some of her friends asked me to go for a walk in the school grounds with them. I said no. I knew Hazel and Alice would be finished their detention, and would be back in our room. I'd have to face them sooner or later, so I might as well get it over with.

Hazel started as soon as I entered the room.

'Did the little baby meet a few nice little boys at the disco? Was the music too loud for her? Did she cry for her Mummy? Did she tell tales on any of her friends and get them into big, big trouble?'

Alice sat up.

'It's getting boring, Hazel. Give it a rest.'

I could hardly believe my ears. Was this the moment I'd been waiting for since this whole nightmare had started?

I turned to Alice.

'Thanks Al,' I said.

She turned away.

'Don't get too excited. I still hate you for getting me into so much trouble. I'm just tired of Hazel going on about it, that's all.'

Hazel gave me an evil look, and went to sit on Alice's bed. She held out her iPod.

'Here, Alice,' she said. 'Listen to this song, it's so funny.'

So they listened to their song, and that was the end of the night that was supposed to be the best night of my whole life.

Chapter twenty-three

When I woke up the next morning, Alice and Hazel were already gone out of the bedroom. I was glad. I was tired of Hazel's sniping and picking on me. I was tired of Alice hating me.

I was glad too that it was the last full day of camp. The next day we'd be going home, and I could start trying to make it up with Alice.

I rolled over in bed and closed my eyes. I tried not to think what my life would be like if Alice stayed fighting with me. We'd been friends for so long, I couldn't imagine life without her. When she moved to Dublin for six months earlier that year, I thought that was the worst thing that could ever happen. I was wrong though. At least then we used to ring each other, and e-mail, and see each other every now and then. This was much, much worse. This was the very worst thing ever. Half the time we'd be living next door to each other, but we might as well be a million miles apart.

Alice and I had been friends since forever. Mum has a gross picture of Alice and me sitting on a rug, and we're both still wearing nappies. (And as if that's not bad enough, my nappy is an ancient, yellow cloth re-usable one, with a huge pin in the middle of it, like something a cartoon baby would wear.)

Alice and I used to watch Barney together, and play Barbies and do Postman Pat jigsaws together. We made our Communion and

Confirmation together.

And now we came away to summer camp together, and we looked forward to it for weeks.

And what did I have to show for my time in summer camp? A fancy dribble in basketball, and no best friend.

I could hear girls moving around, and getting ready to go down for breakfast. There was no time to waste – two more proper breakfasts, and then it was porridge again for me.

I got up and got dressed, and went out into the hallway. I headed for the dining hall. As I got to the second stairs on the way down, I noticed that Hazel was half way up. I sooo did not want to meet her. I looked quickly around, but there was no sign of Alice. In fact there was no sign of anyone else at all. It was just Hazel and me. All of a sudden I felt kind of afraid.

I stopped at the top of the stairs, and pretended I was tying my lace. Hazel came and stood beside me.

'Need some help to tie your laces, little tell-tale baby-girl?'

I didn't answer. I stood up, and set off down the stairs. I'd only gone about three steps, when Hazel was beside me again.

'Oh, I nearly forgot, Alice asked me to tell you something,' she said.

I stopped walking. Why would Alice ask Hazel to bring me a message?

But then, why would Hazel lie?

'So get on with it. Tell me,' I said, trying to sound braver than I felt.

Hazel smiled an evil smile.

'Alice was going to tell you herself, but then she got embarrassed, so I said I'd help her out. I loooove helping people out.'

'Get on with it, Hazel,' I muttered. 'Have you got a message for me or not?'

Hazel smiled again.

'Oh yes, the message. What was it again?'

She stopped for a moment and scratched her

head like she was thinking hard. Then she said,

'Oh yeah, I have it now. It's that Alice hates you.'

Well that was no surprise. I knew that Alice hated me. But I was going to work on that. As soon as we got away from camp, and from Hazel, I was going to explain everything properly. When Alice listened properly, and heard how worried I had been about her, she'd forgive me in the end. I was sure of it. All I had to do was get through one more day.

Hazel seemed disappointed that I didn't react to her so-called message from Alice. She put her face close to mine. I could smell the expensive perfume she always wore.

'Oh yeah,' she said. 'There was something else too. Now what was it?'

She scratched her head, and did her pretend-thinking thing again.

I don't think I had ever in my whole life hated anyone as much as I hated Hazel right then. I always used to hate Melissa, the meanest girl in my class, but she was nothing compared to Hazel.

I felt like punching her pretty face. I wondered what she'd look like if all her perfect white teeth were cracked and broken.

Would her face be so pretty if her nose was all bloody and pushed to one side?

But those were stupid thoughts. I'd never punched anyone in my life, and I wasn't about to start now.

Hazel was still pretending to think. I'd had enough. I set off down the stairs again. Hazel put out her hand and grabbed my arm.

'Don't go, Megan,' she said. 'I haven't got to the best bit of Alice's message yet.'

'So get on with it,' I said. 'I have to go down to breakfast.'

Hazel shook her head.

'Children these days have no patience,' she said.

Then she tossed her head, and spoke all casual,

'Alice asked me to tell you that she never liked you anyway.'

I shook my head.

'That's not true. I know it's not true.'

Hazel smiled her evil smile again.

'Trust me, it's true all right. She said she hates your stupid boring clothes and your silly laugh and the way you're afraid of everything.'

I shook my head again.

'I know you're lying. Alice was always my best friend. Even when she went to live in Dublin we were best friends. She told me so. She always said it. She even sent me e-mails about it.'

Hazel laughed a cruel laugh.

'Yeah, she told me all about that. She told me about how you kept chasing after her. She said she used to go along with it, just because she felt sorry for you.'

I stamped my foot.

'That is so not true. Alice wouldn't say that.

She wouldn't think that.'

Now Hazel smiled the most evil smile of all. Her eyes narrowed as she spoke.

'Don't believe me, do you?'

I shook my head.

'No. Actually I don't.'

'Well believe this then,' she said. 'Alice told me all your little secrets. She told me about your mother the crazy hippy. She told me how your house is like something from an ancient history book. She said you live life like it was still the time of the dinosaurs. She told me how your mother goes on and on and on about the environment, and how you're never allowed to do anything fun. Alice said that everyone in your family is a total loser.'

At last she stopped talking.

I didn't know what to say.

Why would Alice betray me like that?

Why would she tell Hazel, of all people, about my mum?

Maybe what Hazel said was true.

Maybe Alice had never really liked me at all.

Maybe she just hung out with me because I was handy, because I lived next door.

I could feel tears coming to my eyes. Everything went bright and blurry. I soooo did not want Hazel to see that she had made me cry. I shook my arm until she let go of it. Then I pushed past her, and took a few more steps.

Hazel called after me.

'Now you know the truth. Alice has hated you for years. Get over it, why don't you?'

Now rivers of hot tears were pouring down my face. They were dripping down my cheeks and into my mouth. I had to get away from Hazel. I just had to. I had to find someone to help me. I had to find Gloria, Sarah, Sam, or even Alice – anyone who could make Hazel stop.

I started to run down the stairs. Hazel was running after me, taunting me, saying even more horrible things about Alice and me.

It was a huge curving staircase, (the one Alice had slid down on our first day at camp – that day long ago when I had been so happy). The stairs seemed to go on forever, like an enchanted stairs in a fairy-story.

I was almost half-way down, when my foot missed a step, and I stumbled. I reached out and grabbed for the banister. My fingers brushed the smooth wood, but couldn't grip it. I lurched forwards and lost my balance. My shoulder hit the edge of a step. I rolled once, and gave a small scream as my elbow cracked hard against the wall. Things seemed to be happening slowly. One of my shoes fell off, and I could feel my back getting grazed as it slid over a step. I heard a voice calling 'Megan!' and then I rolled again, and hit the tiled floor with a dull thud.

I felt a sudden sharp pain in my head, and then everything went black.

Chapter twenty-four

I was lying on a couch in one of the television rooms when an ambulance pulled up outside. I could see the blue flashing light, and hear the sharp sound of the siren. I wished it would stop – the light was hurting my eyes, and the siren was really hurting my head. For a minute, I wondered who the ambulance was for, then I looked at all the concerned faces gathered around me, and realised that it was for me.

Alice was sitting on the floor next to me, holding my hand so tightly that it hurt. Mrs Duggan was flapping around the room like a demented chicken; Gloria was standing next to me looking very worried. There was no sign of Hazel.

An ambulance man and woman rushed in with a big stretcher on wheels. My head hurt badly, and my elbow was sore, but the stretcher seemed a bit OTT. The men let me sit up on it instead of lying down. On the way out, the stretcher crashed into the door-frame, and bumped my leg, and Gloria said,

'Be careful, isn't she bad enough already?'

The ambulance man laughed, but stopped quickly when he saw Mrs Duggan's face.

Outside in the driveway, Alice clung on to my hand. She pleaded with Mrs Duggan.

'Please let me go with her. *Pleeeeease*. I *have* to go with her. She needs me. She's my very best friend in the whole world.'

I was glad to hear her say that, but the truth

was, my head was hurting so much by then, all I wanted was to be somewhere dark and quiet, and I didn't really care who went with me.

In the end, Mrs Duggan led a crying Alice away, and Gloria came in the ambulance with me. I think Gloria knew that I didn't feel like talking, so as soon as she saw that I was comfortable, she and the ambulance woman had a big long chat about the weather, and holidays in Kerry, and how Gloria managed to keep her hair so shiny.

In the hospital, I was put onto another trolley, and brought into a quiet room. A nice doctor looked into my eyes and ears and asked me loads of questions. After a while he asked me if I knew what date it was.

I thought carefully, before replying.

'No,' I said.

The doctor looked really worried, and I felt as if I had somehow let him down.

'Don't worry,' I said. 'I didn't know what date

it was before I bumped my head either.'

He smiled then.

'You're probably fine,' he said. 'But just to be on the safe side, I think we'd better do a CAT scan.'

Gloria said,

'What does she want a cat scan for – she's a human?' but the doctor didn't seem to think it was very funny. I thought it was funny enough, but didn't dare to laugh in case it would make my head hurt even more.

I had to wait ages and ages for the CAT scan.

'Must be a lot of sick cats in today,' joked Gloria while we were waiting. I felt sorry that no-one was laughing at her jokes, so I laughed a bit even though it made my head hurt.

At last my name was called, and a porter wheeled me into another part of the hospital. The CAT scan was really weird. I was put on a trolley, and told to lie very still. Then the trolley was wheeled into a big metal tube thing, and there were funny noises and lots of bright lights. And just because I'd been told to lie still, I found it very hard to do. Suddenly I felt all fidgety and jumpy, and I badly wanted to scratch my knee. I had headphones on though, and a nice nurse with a lovely soft voice talked to me and tried to distract me until the whole thing was over.

When I was wheeled out of the x-ray room, Mum and Dad and Rosie were there waiting for me. They all raced over, and Mum and Dad kissed and hugged me as well as they could since I was still lying down. Rosie didn't kiss or hug me – she was too busy making funny faces at her reflection in the shiny wheels of the trolley.

Mum started crying then, and saying she should never have let me go to camp, that I was too young, and that girls my age were safer at home where their parents could keep an eye on them.

Dad hugged her though and said that most accidents happen in the home anyway.

Then Mum put her hand over her mouth and said she thought she'd left the iron on, as she'd been ironing when the call came that I'd had the accident. Then there was a big panic, and she had to phone her friend, who lives up the road from us, and tell her where the spare key was hidden, and ask her to make sure that the house wasn't burning down. And Dad said she wouldn't need the key to see if the house was burning down or not. And Mum got cross and said Dad could never see the bigger picture. (Whatever that means.) Then Rosie's finger got caught in one of the trolley wheels, and she screeched for ages, and all the nurses made a big fuss of her, because she's so small and cute. And every time the nurses lost interest in her she screeched some more, just so they'd come back. After a while a nurse brought in a big box of coloured plasters, and said Rosie could choose one, and Rosie got so excited she accidentally knocked the box out of the nurses hand, and the plasters went all over the floor making it look like there had been some kind of explosion. And in the end, I felt a bit left out of things, lying on my trolley, until I felt like shouting *Hey, I'm the patient here, is anyone going to pay me any attention?*

I was brought back down to the nice doctor. He put on his glasses, and looked at the chart, which was clipped on to the end of my trolley.

'Hmmm,' he said after a while. 'Everything looks fine, but I think you'd better stay in hospital overnight, for observation.'

I didn't much like the sound of that. Was someone going to sit next to me all the time, watching me?

In the end, it wasn't so bad. I was just put into a nice room with just one bed in it, and a nurse peeped in and checked on me every hour or so. All the nurses were really nice to me, and made a big fuss of me, which was just what I needed after so many days of feeling sorry for myself.

Mum insisted on staying with me. I thought

that was a bit stupid. She's always imagining bad things, but what on earth did she think was going to happen to me in a hospital? And after all, I was twelve years old. Mum had that look in her eye, though, and I knew there was no point in arguing.

Mum wouldn't leave me, even for a minute, so Dad and Rosie went to find a shop to buy me night clothes and a toothbrush. Dad somehow managed to buy me pyjamas that fitted me, and were nice. The toothbrush had Barbie on it. Rosie smiled.

'I picked it specially for you,' she said.

Dad bought me loads of books too. My head still hurt, and I couldn't possibly read, but I didn't like to hurt his feelings by saying so. Then we all sat and looked at each other and talked about stupid stuff until the nurse came in and said, 'bed-time,' which I thought was a bit strange, as I was the only patient, and I was in bed already. Then Dad stood up, and he and

Rosie kissed me, and went to stay the night with one of Dad's old friends from college.

The nurses kept telling Mum that there was a spare bed in the family room, up the hall, but Mum wouldn't hear of using it.

'If my daughter needs me during the night,' she said. 'I intend to be right here by her side. I'm not taking any chances.'

I thought that was a bit stupid, and I felt kind of guilty tucked up in a big, high, comfortable bed with starchy sheets and loads of blankets, while Mum was curled up uncomfortably on an arm-chair next to me. Still though, I woke up loads of times during the night, and it was nice to look over, and see that Mum was by my side, minding me.

Chapter twenty-five

In the morning a nurse I hadn't seen before came into the room.

'Well, you're looking all bright and breezy,' she said in a friendly voice.

She read my chart, checked my temperature and smoothed out my sheets, humming as she did so. Just then, Mum uncurled herself from her armchair, and stood up. As usual, her hair was sticking out everywhere, and her dress looked like it had never been within a hundred metres of an iron.

The nurse looked at her.

'Oh my God,' she said. 'Look at the state of you. Why don't you run along to the family room and tidy yourself up?'

I felt really bad, because the nurse was trying to be nice, and how could she possibly know that Mum always looks like that?

Poor Mum didn't say anything, but she politely went off to the family room as the nurse had instructed. When she came back, looking exactly the same as before, the nurse sighed and said,

'Oh, well. Can't be helped. A night at home will do you all a world of good, I'm sure.'

I was glad when her beeper beeped, and she had to go out before she hurt Mum's feelings any more.

By this time, my head-ache was better, so I had time to examine my other injuries. My back was all scraped, and my elbow and my ankle were badly bruised. Nothing hurt too badly though.

After a while, the nice doctor came in. He read

my chart, and looked into my eyes.

'Good news – no real damage,' he said to Mum. 'A few days rest and she'll be as good as new.'

'What a wonderful doctor you are,' said Mum. She looked so happy, I thought she was going to kiss him. He must have thought so too, because he left the room very quickly, muttering something about an emergency in another part of the hospital.

A few minutes later, a nurse came in with a big bundle of forms for Mum to sign. While Mum was doing the paperwork, I got dressed. It felt a bit strange, putting on the same clothes that I'd put on the day before, all ready for my last full day at camp.

When we were ready, Mum phoned Dad and asked him to come and pick us up, and my unexpected visit to hospital was over.

Before going home, we had to go out to the summer camp to pick up my stuff. On the way,

Mum and Dad kept asking me stuff about the camp.

'Did you enjoy it?'

'Were the other kids nice?'

'Did you make any new friends?'

'Are you sorry it's over?'

I didn't know how to answer all these hard questions. After all the drama of the fall down the stairs, and the trip to hospital, the fight with Alice seemed very trivial and very long ago. It seemed like it had happened in a different world.

Anyway, there was no way I was telling Mum and Dad about the row. Anyone who thinks that it's only elephants who never forget obviously hasn't met my mum, *and* she's a world champion at holding grudges.

When I was in senior infants, a boy in my class kicked me, and now, more than six years later, Mum still gives him evil looks whenever we pass him in the street.

So I just smiled and half-answered their

questions, and because I'd been in hospital they smiled back and didn't give me a hard time.

*   *   *

When we got to the camp, we met Gloria in the hallway. She gave me a big hug that really hurt my scraped back and my sore elbow. She whispered in my ear.

'Would you like me to tell your folks about all that bad stuff between you and Alice?'

I shook my head as hard as I could, considering that I felt like I was being hugged by a large and very friendly bear.

Gloria let me go, and looked at me a bit doubtfully.

'Maybe it's something they need to know,' she suggested. 'I needn't tell them all the details. I could just say there was a bit of a row.'

That would have been a total disaster. If Mum heard that her precious daughter had 'a bit of a row' with her best friend, it would have been a very, very big deal. She wouldn't have stopped digging until she knew every detail of who had said what, and when, and even what they were wearing when they said it.

Just then I was rescued by a huge shriek.

'Meg! You're back! Are you OK?'

It was Alice, who came racing down the stairs almost as fast as I had fallen down it the day before. She grabbed me and gave me a huge hug. I tried not to cry out in pain – too many more of those hugs and I'd be back with the nice doctor, getting my sore back treated.

When Alice finally let me go, Gloria grinned at me.

'Looks like everything's OK again.'

I nodded happily.

'Yes, Gloria,' I said. 'Everything's just fine.'

Mrs Duggan appeared then. She went over to Mum and Dad and shook their hands and smiled. I'd never seen her smile before, and was surprised that the muscles in her face knew what to do.

'Mr and Mrs Sheehan,' she said. 'So nice to meet you. And poor little Megan. Such an awful thing to happen. It was a complete accident, you know that, don't you?'

Mum didn't answer Mrs Duggan.

'Is this where you fell, Megan?' she asked me.

I nodded.

'Almost from the top,' I said proudly, exaggerating a bit.

Mum went so pale, I had to correct myself.

'Well, not really almost the top. It was more like half way down.'

Mum still didn't look very well.

'Well, actually, it was only the last few steps,' I lied, and at last Mum looked like she wasn't going to faint.

I could see that she was looking at the stairs to see if there were any dangers that she wouldn't have allowed in her own house. She seemed happy though, as there were no fraying carpets, or bumpy steps or shaky banisters.

She smiled at Mrs Duggan.

'Of course it was a complete accident,' she said. 'It could have happened anywhere.'

Now that it looked like Mum and Dad weren't planning to sue her, Mrs Duggan relaxed a bit, and she actually smiled again.

'And Megan's such a sweet girl,' she said. 'Everyone loved her here. She's a credit to you. She got on so well with the other girls, you just wouldn't believe it.'

Mum and Dad smiled, enjoying the praise. Luckily they didn't see Gloria winking at me behind their backs. I winked back.

Dad looked at his watch.

'I really ought to show my face at work some time today,' he said. 'Maybe we could move along a bit here.'

Mum nodded.

'OK. Megan, do you want a hand with packing up your things?'

Before I could answer, Alice stepped forward.

'It's OK,' she said. 'I'll help her.'

Mrs Duggan turned to Mum and Dad.

'Why don't you join me for a cup of tea while you're waiting?'

Mum smiled at her.

'That would be lovely. Do you have any white tea? Or even green would do.'

Mrs Duggan shook her head.

'Actually, no, Mrs Sheehan,' she said. 'I'm afraid I have neither green nor white tea.'

'Oh well,' Mum said. 'Don't worry. I have loads.'

She put her ugly patchwork handbag down on the floor. (I noticed with horror that the bag was made from a few of Rosie's old summer dresses.) She rooted around inside it, pulling out all kinds of embarrassing rubbish, and spreading it around the floor. At last she said,

'Here it is,' as she held up a raggy old bag of teabags that looked as if it had been in her bag for a few hundred years.

Mum smiled at Mrs Duggan.

'And there's plenty. Lots of lovely healthy anti-oxidants for everyone.'

Mrs Duggan gave her a weak look, and led the way to her study.

Alice and I grinned at each other, then she took my good arm and we went up the camp stairs for the very last time.

Chapter twenty-six

When we got into our room, Alice closed the door behind us. She gave me another big hug. Then we both sat on my bed.

'Can you ever forgive me?' she asked.

'For what?'

I knew what she wanted me to forgive her for, of course, but it seemed like the right answer.

And besides, a little bit of me wanted to hear her say out loud what she'd done. Just so we could get it all out in the open, and over with.

Alice sighed.

'Where should I start? Can you forgive me for being the worst friend ever? For being the meanest person in the history of the world? For—'

I put up my hand to stop her.

'First, can you forgive me for telling on you?'

Alice nodded.

'Of course I can.'

Still there was more I needed to say.

'I *was* jealous, I'll admit that. I was really, really jealous of you and Hazel going off on a date together. But I would never have told on you just to get you into trouble. I'd never do anything like that to you.'

Alice nodded.

'I know. I understand that now.'

I went on.

'I was just so afraid. I never thought of

something simple like that you'd missed the bus. I thought something really awful had happened to you. I kept thinking of bad things.'

Alice gave a sudden laugh.

'Are you turning into your mother by any chance?'

I made a face.

'I hope not. Are you turning into yours?'

Alice made an even worse face, and we both laughed.

Then Alice became serious again.

'I wanted to make it up with you after the first day. I was all ready to talk to you, and be your friend again. But Hazel stopped me. She told me all kinds of bad stuff about you, and she made it all sound so convincing. I couldn't resist her. I knew I was being unfair to you, but I couldn't stop myself. It was almost like I'd forgotten how to think for myself.'

Suddenly I thought of something.

'You told Hazel stories about my mum. You

told all about the environmental stuff. You made her sound even crazier than she really is.'

Alice put her head down.

'Did Hazel tell you that?'

I nodded.

'Why did you do that? I don't mind when you joke with me about that stuff, but why did you share it with Hazel, of all people?'

Alice gave a big sigh.

'It's not as bad as it sounds. Honestly. It happened on one of the first days we were here – one of the days when I still thought that you, me and Hazel were going to be friends. Hazel was mocking behind your back, because you don't have a mobile phone, or an iPod, or any of that stuff. So I told her what your mum is like. I tried to make it sound like your mum is funny. I didn't mean to make her sound crazy. And then I said that even though your mum's like that, that you were really nice. I said it wasn't your fault, and that it didn't matter. I said that cool stuff doesn't

234

matter when you're as nice as you are.'

I made a face.

'Hazel didn't mention that bit.'

Alice shook her head.

'Yeah, I bet she didn't. But I made a mistake. I shouldn't have said anything about your mum. After all, with a mum like mine, who am I to mock anyone else?'

We both laughed again. Then we both stopped suddenly.

'About yesterday …' began Alice, '… I saw you on the stairs with Hazel. What exactly happened? Did she … ?'

I knew what it was that she was afraid to ask. I shook my head.

'No, she didn't push me. She was saying all that mean stuff, and I was trying so hard to get away, and I was crying, and I … well I suppose I just fell.'

Alice looked relieved.

'I was downstairs. I came around the corner,

and I saw you tumbling. And I tried to save you. I ran towards the bottom of the stairs. I thought I might be able to break your fall. But I tripped over my shoe-lace, and I fell.'

'Did you hurt yourself?'

She shrugged.

'I banged my arm, but it doesn't matter.' As she spoke, she pulled up her sleeve, and I could see that most of her arm was black and blue. It was much worse than any of my injuries.

I touched her arm as gently as I could, and she flinched.

'But Alice, that's really bad. You should let someone look at it.'

She pulled down her sleeve again.

'Nah. It's fine. It's only a bruise, and last night, when I knew you were in the hospital, and I knew it was partly my fault, I was so glad that I was hurting too.'

I had to laugh.

'You are so crazy sometimes,' I said.

Alice smiled.

'Whatever. I'm just sorry I didn't manage to save you.'

Suddenly I remembered.

'Did you call my name?'

She nodded.

'Yeah. And I rubbed your arm until help came. In the end it was all I could do.'

Suddenly I remembered something else.

'Where *is* Hazel, anyway?' I asked.

'She had to leave first thing. For her big trip to America, remember? I didn't even say goodbye to her. I couldn't. I saw her at the top of the stairs. I knew she'd been bullying you again, and she didn't even look sorry that you were hurt.'

'It doesn't matter,' I said. 'I don't care about Hazel any more.'

Alice stamped her foot, making me smile. She'd never have done that babyish thing in front of Hazel.

'It *does* matter,' she said. 'I was so totally stupid.

I actually liked Hazel. I wanted to be her friend. I watched her being mean to you, and I still liked her. How could I have let that happen?'

I shrugged.

'I don't know. But like I said, it doesn't matter. I've forgotten about Hazel already.'

'About who?' asked Alice, and we both laughed.

Then I remembered yet another thing.

'What about Lee?' I asked.

Alice thought for a long while, and then she said.

'Know what? I didn't even like him all that much. He was a bit too smart. A bit too sure of himself. He kept telling jokes, and half of them weren't even funny.'

'I bet you laughed anyway,' I said.

Alice looked ashamed.

'Afraid so,' she said, in a mock-tragic voice.

We both giggled, and then Alice continued.

'I just liked the idea of having a boyfriend for

the first time ever, you know?'

'But what about Eliot?'

Alice went red.

'I made him up. Well, I suppose I didn't actually make him up. He did exist, and he was totally cute, but he never liked me. He liked one of the girls in my class, and I was jealous. I made up the stuff about going out with him to impress what's-her-name.'

Neither of us said anything for a minute, and then Alice remembered something.

'Hey, what about Sam?'

Now it was my turn to go red.

'What about him?'

'He likes you. And you like him, don't you?'

I nodded. No point in lying now.

'It doesn't matter anyway,' I said. 'I won't see him ever again.'

Alice sighed.

'Such a pity. Still, you met him before I met Lee, so when we're old and grey, you can always say that you had the first boyfriend.'

I smiled. It might not have been strictly true, but it was nice to pretend to be first at something.

Suddenly I looked at my watch. I jumped up.

'Dad will be dancing jigs downstairs. We'd better pack up quickly.'

Alice helped me to put my stuff back into my rucksack. She didn't pack her own stuff, she was going to wait on for the camp closing ceremony that afternoon, and come home by bus later. Mum wouldn't let me stay for the closing ceremony, and in a way, I didn't mind. I'd had enough excitement over the past few days.

When all my stuff was in my rucksack, Alice reached into the wardrobe, and pulled out the turquoise top. She folded it carefully, and put it on top of my clothes.

'You can keep it,' she said.

I stroked the soft fabric.

'Are you sure?'

She nodded.

'Sure I'm sure. Just give it a good wash before you wear it – what's-her-name had it last.'

We laughed again.

On the way downstairs, we met Sarah. She gave me a hug – a gentle one that hardly hurt my back at all.

'I'm so glad you weren't badly hurt,' she said.

Then she pulled a pen and paper from her sports bag, and wrote down her phone number.

'Text me,' she said.

I didn't reply. As the only girl in the world without a mobile phone, texting would have been a bit difficult. Sarah saw my face.

'Ooops. Sorry,' she said. She took back the paper and wrote down her address. 'Write to me then.'

I nodded. I knew I would. If it hadn't been for Sarah, things would have been a lot worse for me that week.

Just as Alice and I got to the bottom of the

stairs, Sam appeared. I could feel my face going red, but it didn't matter, as his skin had suddenly taken on a distinct pink colour.

'We all thought you were dead,' he said.

'I'm not,' was the only stupid thing I could think of saying.

Sam laughed.

'I'm glad,' he said, and suddenly I felt warm and happy.

'And don't forget,' he said. 'If you ever need me to spit in anyone's drink, I'm only a phone call away.'

We all laughed, and then there was an embarrassing silence.

'Er … I'd better go,' said Sam. He gave me a quick hug, and walked quickly off towards the dining hall.

Alice and I went outside. It was a beautiful day. Mum and Dad and Rosie were standing next to the car, waiting for me.

Alice turned to me.

'I'll be home around seven, OK? I'll call for you then.'

Then she hugged me again. She had tears in her eyes.

Dad shook his head.

'What are you girls like? You'd never think you'd just had three wonderful long weeks together.'

Alice and I looked at each other and smiled.

'Have you said good-bye to all your friends?' asked Mum. 'What about that pushy girl with the blonde hair. What was her name again?'

Alice and I spoke together.

'We forget,' we said, and then we stood in the driveway of the summer camp, and laughed until we cried.

THE 'ALICE & MEGAN' SERIES
BY

Judi Curtin

HAVE YOU READ THEM ALL?

Don't miss all the great books about
Alice & Megan:

Alice Next Door
Alice Again
Don't Ask Alice
Alice in the Middle
Bonjour Alice
Alice & Megan Forever
Alice to the Rescue
Viva Alice!
Alice & Megan's Cookbook

Best friends NEED to be together. Don't they?

Poor Megan! Not alone is she stuck with totally uncool parents, and a little sister who is too cute for words, but now her best friend, Alice, has moved away. Now Megan has to go to school and face the dreaded Melissa all on her own.

The two friends hatch a risky plot to get back together. But can their secret plan work?

It's mid-term break and Megan's off to visit Alice.

Megan is hoping for a nice trouble-free few days with her best friend. No such luck! She soon discovers that Alice is once again plotting and scheming.
It seems that Alice's mum Veronica has a new boyfriend. The plan is to discover who he is, and to get rid of him!

Alice and Megan
are together again!

They are both looking forward to their Confirmation,
especially as their two families are going out to
dinner together to celebrate.
But not even a meal can be simple when Alice is
around as she decides to hatch a plan to get her
parents back together ...

Best friends forever?

Megan can't wait to go away to Summer Camp with
Alice!
It will be fantastic — no organic porridge, no school,
nothing but fun! But when Alice makes friends with
Hazel, Megan begins to feel left out. Hazel's pretty,
sophisticated and popular, and Alice seems to think
she's amazing.
Is Megan going to lose her very best friend?

Sunshine & yummy French food — sounds like the perfect holiday!

Megan's really looking forward to the summer holidays — her whole family is going to France, and best of all Alice is coming too! But when Alice tries to make friends with a local French boy things begin to get very interesting ...

Alice and Megan are starting secondary school.

New subjects, new teachers and new friends — it's going to take a bit of getting used to.

And when Megan meets Marcus, the class bad-boy who's always in trouble, but doesn't seem to care, things really start to get complicated.

At least she has Home Ec class with Alice — the worst cook in the school — to look forward to, so school's not all bad!

Winning is a good thing, isn't it?

Everyone in first year is really excited about the big prize in the English essay competition — four months in France — and Alice has a good chance of winning.

Megan loves writing essays, but she doesn't want to win — go away for four months alone, no way! She doesn't want Alice to go either — why would anyone want to go abroad without her best friend? But Alice seems determined to win ...

Alice & Megan's
COOKBOOK

Get cooking with Alice & Megan!

Alice and Megan are writing a cookbook. But Alice is not the world's the greatest cook ... so could it be a recipe for disaster? Well, not with Megan's help - as well as advice (whether the girls want it or not!) from Megan's mum, little sister Rosie, Miss Leonard, the Home Economics Teacher ...

This fun-filled cookbook is packed with fantastic recipes!
Brilliant Breakfasts . Lucky Lunchboxes . Super Snacks .
Marvellous Main Courses . Delicious Desserts . Cakes & Cookies.

VISIT JUDI CURTIN'S WEBSITE!

Latest Judi news, new books, events
Exclusive sneak peeks
'Ask Judi'
... and much more!

www.obrien.ie